Henry Morford

Rhymes of an editor

Henry Morford

Rhymes of an editor

ISBN/EAN: 9783337271725

Printed in Europe, USA, Canada, Australia, Japan

Cover: Foto ©Andreas Hilbeck / pixelio.de

More available books at **www.hansebooks.com**

RHYMES

OF

AN EDITOR.

—

INCLUDING "ALMOST."

—

By HENRY MORFORD,

AUTHOR OF "RHYMES OF TWENTY YEARS."

LONDON:

E. MOXON, SON & Co., DOVER STREET,

AND 1. AMEN CORNER, PATERNOSTER ROW.

NEW YORK:

SHELDON & Co., 677, BROADWAY.

1873.

PRINTED BY TAYLOR AND CO.,
LITTLE QUEEN STREET, LINCOLN'S INN FIELDS.

A RHYME PREFATORY.

At fifty years 'tis time, calm thought reminds,
   The bound of youth's producing-power to measure,
And seek, thenceforth, that joy the old man finds
   In counting and exhibiting his treasure.

Some portion may be counterfeit and base;
   Some pieces may be old, worn, clipped, uncurrent;
And yet if they display the minted face,
   His pride will have at least a show of warrant.

And if, in earlier days, a previous hoard,*
   Thrown out before the world, at daring venture,
Has been received as something wisely stored
   And met few words of even kindly censure,—

     * " Rhymes of Twenty Years "—New York, 1859.

Then may the old man, so much labour done,
  Be not unwise or over-sanguine reckoned,
In hazarding the gain already won
  In his first venture, by a bolder second.

So to the kindly world whose first applause
  Has made all after-labour lighter, sweeter,
These Rhymes go out, to plead their humble cause,
  In truest earnest, if in halting metre.

At worst, this thought may soften all the rest:
  At fifty, the romantic day's completed;
And, meet what fate it may, this second test
  Is final, and will never be repeated.

LONDON,
    July 25th, 1873.

TABLE OF CONTENTS.

I.

ALMOST.

ALMOST.

L'ENVOI.

Man's earth-born patent let the record be—
The hair's-breadth misses of humanity.

I.

SINCE first the startled words Agrippa spoke
Upon the ears of God's apostle broke :—
" Almost, oh Christian, thou persuadest me
A follower of the Nazarene to be ! "—
Since Greek Anceus' overlaboured slave
That solemn warning to his tyrant gave :
" The wine-cup may be almost at the lips
Yet dashed to earth before the holder sips ! "— ·
Ay, centuries before—since first the soul
Learned that it had a duty and a goal,—
O'er all the years of time—half sprite—half ghost—
Has loomed that strange, wild, pregnant word—
    " *Almost !* "

A drop of gall in every pleasant cup ;
A sword above the head when tyrants sup ;
A Mordecai that sits in every gate,
When hasty Hamans for their triumph wait ;
A sad reminder that, for weal or woe,
"Thus far, no farther, mortal, shalt thou go !"
Is both the doom and bliss of all below.

II.

Not all a blessing—not alone a ban—
This curb and boundary to the fate of man ;—
This line, so delicate and yet so broad,
Between the attributes and works of God.
For while no limit stays the hand Divine,
Our mortal energy must own the line ;
And while the Eternal wing beats strong and free
Through the blue ether of immensity—
The feebler pinion that awhile may soar,
Sinks, tired at last, upon Time's bounded shore.
The action that has motion, power and birth
In minds created and in limbs of earth,—
Sprung from the noblest hopes of human good,
Or fed with hate's unblest and poison food,—
Born in a curse or nurtured in a prayer—
Be what it will, the mark of time is there !
A year—an hour—may bring the welcome fruit ;
A year—an hour—may blight it at the root.

It *may be*, but it has no power beyond,
Though hopes be eager and though hearts be fond:
The perfect *All* spans the great arch of Heaven—
The imperfect *Almost* to man's brow is given!

III.

So, though the wish may force, the will may urge,—
All our lives long we only tread some verge,—
The border of some pleasant promised land,
Where eyes may feast, but feet may never stand.
Our boyhood's butterflies, whose spangled wings
Seemed as a type of all alluring things,
Mocking the jewels and the robes of kings—
We hunted them till foot and heart grew sore;
We grasped, and missed them by an inch—no more!
The shape has changed; and many a weary year
That butterfly-pursuit has cost us dear:—
The boy no more, his young heart pit-a-pat,
Chasing the insect with his ragged hat,
Snuffing the fragrance golden summer yields,
Hearing the sweet birds singing o'er the fields,—
But full-grown man—the master of his will,
Proud of his strength and glorying in his skill,—
His butterfly a love—a hope—a name,
The miser's lucre or the wreath of fame,—
A kingly bauble, or a patriot's blow
Right stoutly aimed to lay oppression low:—

We *almost* grasp them : ere life's sun has set,
We know—we feel that we shall grasp them yet !
And so we shall !—grasp them, if not before,
In that contentment—*needing them no more !*

IV.

Pictures, like phantoms, drawn from every stage
Of life's experience, start upon the page ;
Pictures, whose very features, dim and faint,
Show the imperfect hand that dares to paint ;
Subject and work the dim and unattained
Toward which the world in every age has strained.
But once, in centuries' lapse, some master hand,
With heaven's own gorgeous colours at command—
All time his palette, and his canvas broad
The human heart wherever cheered or awed—
But once, in every age, some century-flower
Perfuming all creation for an hour—
"A little lower than the angels" are,
But throned above our nature like a star,—
Paints us such pictures, gorgeous, true and rare,
It almost seems Omnipotence is there.
Alas ! the nearer heaven their glories reach,
Still darker spot and blemish show on each ;
And we may joy at last—if joy it be—
What weak hands draw still weaker eyes may see !
The angels read, but read no vellum scroll;
The blots *they* weep are on the human soul !

v.

Look how they change—one vast kaleidoscope:.
Averted evil into broken hope ;—
Good, almost ripened into golden prime,
Just nipped and rotted ere its perfect time ;—
Wrong, loss and ruin, ere expended all,
In drops of mercy seeming yet to fall.—
The proof not only that our finite hands
Can neither force nor forge the fettering bands,—
But that our dim eyes even fail to see
If curse or blessing in the check there be!
Both Janus-faced are happiness and woe—
We see one face, and think the whole we know ;
We see another—own ourselves deceived,
But this—ah ! this at last may be believed !
So each, his partial wisdom fondly nursed,
Mistakes the hundredth as he did the first !
Yet, till the trumpet sounds the final call,
Vain hopes will rise, and needless tears will fall ;
And hands will write what, better than their tales,
Will prove how human effort faints and fails !

vi.

A solemn subject—else the mind might draw
Droll humours from the slips of love and law,—
See the hot lover, in successful suit,
Just ruined by a tightly-fitting boot ;—

Or the pert lawyer, in a pliant court,
Balked by a simple witness, caught for sport ;—
Or tonnish lady, throned on fashion's height,
In one crushed bonnet-box demolished quite ;—
Or ripened maiden, all her prospects fair,
Kept from a husband by her truant hair ;—
Or managing mamma, three lions caged,
Losing them all, to have the fourth engaged ;—
Or wily jockey, on the racing-course,
Kept from his winnings by his winning horse ;—
These, and a thousand others, gay and grave,
Float by us, like the bubbles on the wave :
We fain would catch them, as they glitter past,
But they are only bubbles, at the last !
Beneath them, in the sea of sadder thought,
The pictures lie that must be deftly caught.

VII.

Low lies the glow of evening on the sea—
Sunshine and swell in dalliance soft and free ;
The wind a zephyr, and the sun a smile ;
The air one fragrance from some tropic isle.
Such seas, beyond our world of storm and ice,
Might break upon the shores of paradise :
Such breezes may the immortal cheeks have fanned,
Beside the rivers of the Perfect Land.
The sun is kissing white and spreading sails,
Whose broken shadow far to leeward trails :

It glistens on the stout ship's wave-worn sides
That on that sea of liquid glory rides.
An hundred anxious hearts that vessel bears—
Their fears, their hopes, their curses and their prayers.
Exiles for liberty, for pride, or crime,
Away from native lands to some new clime;—
Light-hearted voyagers, running travel's race,
Who find no home but in a change of place;
And some there are, returning o'er the waves
From years of absence to their fathers' graves—
To sunny curls, so often smoothed in vain,
And eyes that o'er the deep must watch and strain.
The cord that drew them home, through passing years,
Has seemed to tighten, wetted with their tears,
Till a dull pain at last the thought has grown,
And nightly visions have this scope alone,—
Till o'er the wave some fate appears to call,
And they obey it though they peril all!

VIII.

Oh, little worlds—ye speeding, white-winged ships!
What interests bear you on your varied trips!
What changing nations in a little space
Find in your narrow walls awhile their place!
How many hearts—a stranger each to each—
Hold you at once in anxious thought and speech!
How senseless plank and stolid iron bear
A sacred task that wraps them round with prayer!

And how, when wisdom or when skill may fail,
Or human might bends low to wave or gale—
Your bleaching ribs, on some deserted coast,
May bear the weird, wild horror of a ghost,
Or make the eyes, years hence, that o'er them bend,
Drop tears, as o'er the body of a friend !

IX.

This evening hush—who does not feel its power ?
Who does not drink the glory of the hour ?
Over the bulwark leaning, there is one
Whose eyes have closely scanned the setting sun,—
Whose brain seems weaving into pleasant thought
The rosy tints in far-off cloud-land wrought.
About the westering sun, for many days,
Have hung and lingered golden cloud and haze ;
And but this morning, like a frightened thing
A land-bird passed with frail and faltering wing :
To-day a branch whose berries seemed to burn
With fresh red lustre, floated by astern :
Another day—or life-long omens miss—
Green waves of home the plunging prow shall kiss.
Another day—and, joy beyond command,
Shall ring the pleasing cry : " Land ho ! the land !"—
Sound empty as the tropics' echoing shell
To those who tread the soil they love so well :
Sound full and pregnant with a maddened glee
To the tired watchers on a broadening sea.

Already hearts beat high, and faces glow,
And the small world are all astir below,—
As under June's sweet sunshine broad and warm
The old hive buzzes ere the young bees swarm.

X.

What sees the gazer o'er those leagues of tide—
The broad high browed—the keen and anxious eyed?
Against the bulwark leaning close he stands,
The rail firm gripped within his nervous hands,
And all beside him—all behind him—lost
In those long lines of waves so slowly crossed.
The face once fair and smooth is furrowed deep;
Beneath the eyes dull leaden shadows sleep;
And threads of silver—loomed by years of care—
Bind age and youth together in his hair.

XI.

A life half wasted and a life regained;
A reputation cleared, once dimmed and stained;
A fortune sunken in the sea of wrong,
Then rescued by a diver stern and strong;
Exile that dwarfed home's dear and sacred thought;
Home-tortures that a prayer for exile brought;
Pulses made languid by ascetic rule,
Then heated by the licence of the fool;
Heat, cold, repletion, hunger, rust and toil;
Mist from all seas and dust from every soil

Beating on brow and thickening in the brain,
Till rest and labour grew alike a pain;
Hope, torture, pride, ambition and despair—
Look on his brow—all have a record there.

XII.

What sees he? That home-land which o'er the main
Has drawn him ever with an exile's chain;—
That land from which, in search of fame and gold,
He parted young and lingered on till old;—
That dear home-land to which, with weary track,
His day's-work done, he brings his earnings back.
Home—*almost* home! At home the gold has need;
The hard-won honours there must bear their meed,
Love's chain be linked again before too late,
And energy compare accounts with fate.
Home—*almost* home! A few more leagues of sea,
And this dim " almost" shall the perfect be!—
So thinks the watcher, as with one long sigh
From the wide waters he withdraws his eye,
Feels how the last drop brims the cup of tears—
How the last hours of waiting grow to years,—
And slow descends, as evening gathers deep,
To bridge his gulf of waiting o'er with sleep.—
Sleep—that has mines and millions at command—
Sleep—that holds heaven within her poppied hand—
Hides the rough " now " in graves so dark and low,⎫
Builds up the future's pinnacles of snow,⎬
And opes the golden gates of " long ago."⎭

XIII.

But sleep not long, oh ! watcher for the land !
For clouds no bigger than a human hand
May shroud a sky between the dusk and dawn—
A fear foreshadowed—then a last hope gone.
The sails are reefed at midnight : ere the day
Before the gale the scared ship flies away,
Her course unknown, unguided, lost and blind—
Black sea before her, maddened foam behind.
The sleeper wakes—to feel the plunging roll ;—
To find his ship a steed, with death the goal ;
To hear the loud command, the oath, the shriek ;
To feel the warm blood freeze in limb and cheek ;
To join the last fierce cry that rings to heaven
When spars fall toppling and when planks are riven
To lie, as braver men have lain before,
A lifeless, drifting sea-weed on the shore.
Oh, " almost " of the present ! who shall dare
To say what hue the perfect time may wear ?
Or who shall wish that painful present, past,
Undreaming what may follow, at the last ?
Oh, watcher by the gunwale ! in that hour
When he who waited fruit despised the flower—
Thou hadst the most to boast—the least to mourn :
The flower was all—the fruit was never borne.
Almost at home, with honour, life and gold ;
Wrecked, lost and ruined ere the night was told.

XIV.

Lost, but not dead! Almost the fate befell
No living tongue the good ship's end should tell;
And glad the wanderer's dear and deadly foe
Reads o'er the tale that tells a rival low,
Blesses the storm that came in happy time
To baffle innocence and comfort crime:
Blesses too soon—what form is standing there
With torn, wet clothing, massed and sanded hair?
With blood-shot eye, with pale and haggard cheek
And lips that murmur when they fain would speak?
A ragged beggar, but with bones and nerves
That yet may deal the fate which crime deserves.
Do the wild seas give up their dead? Not so!
But lost or living only God may know.
The cold, damp sea-weed on the wet beach sands
Was warmed to life by tried and trusty hands.
Almost his goal of triumph grasped as found,—
Twice came the limit—once with mercy crowned:
Thank Heaven that he was ONLY *almost* drowned!

XV.

The sea-mist lifts, and shows a battle plain
Where armies shrink 'neath storms of iron rain,—
Where Death the reaper holds his slaves at call,
Ambition mows and human harvests fall.
In twenty battles has yon man of blood,
Baton or glass in hand, unblenching stood:

In twenty battles—twenty fought and done—
That player with human lives has won—still won.
The last poor remnant of a falling race
Here stand, to meet their tyrant face to face,
To look their last on pleasant earth and sky,
Strike their last blow for native land—and die!
Almost the purple wraps his rugged limbs;
Almost in diamond waves his forehead swims:
One effort more, and they are at his feet,
Begging the mercy conquered nations meet!
Charge, squadrons! open fire, each serried line!
And give fresh feasts to Mars, with blood for wine!

XVI.

Almost the warrior—conqueror—proudly treads
His path of empire paved with human heads;
Almost—ha! what is this? One poor old man—
Six sons all dead in whom his life-blood ran,—
Six sons, who one by one on honour's field
Have yielded life for rights they would not yield;—
That poor old man, a bare and sapless tree,
With bleeding wounds where stout limbs used to be,—
Has yet that strength the deadly tube to range,—
The strength for one last luxury—revenge.
Beside a crumbling wall that up the hill
Runs its long course, he crouches, close and still.
No serpent subtler writhes its sinuous way
When mists of glamour gather round its prey;

No evil habit steals with gentler force
Along the veins that trust its treacherous course.
His white head bare, his body stooping low,
The old man steals upon the nation's foe,
The gathered lightnings of an outraged land
All sleeping in the pellet 'neath his hand.
He crouches closer—drops upon his knee—
Peers o'er the ruin—shakes his right arm free—
Covers the tyrant with his deadly aim,
And pours, with prayer half curse, the jetting flame.
That moment waves the arm to point the charge,
Opening the tender arm-pit as a targe,
And there the bullet enters with a thud,
Soaking his vestment with the spouting blood,
Crashing, as crashed of old Goliath's stone,
Through blood and life—through sinew, flesh and bone.
One wild, fierce clutch at thin and empty air,
One reel—the conqueror's saddle-seat is bare,
And stark and stiff, his white face to the sun,
His catalogue of victories is done.

XVII.

Almost a ruined people—see the dawn
Of freedom coming when their scourge is gone.
That poor, down-trodden nation rise once more
When fades the shadow of the name *he* bore ;—
Fight freedom's weary fight with stubborn will,
With different chance and ever-varying skill,

Sometimes with victory's banners on the air
And grateful shouts repaying long despair,
Almost enfranchised : then the night comes down,
And hostile forces swarm through vale and town,
And in the mountain passes, starved and cold,
The life of freedom keeps its only hold :
Almost enslaved.   And so the record goes
Of nearly every nation's natal throes—
The darkest hour ere light the morning fires ;
The brightest flash ere the last hope expires.

XVIII.

Narrow the vision from the great wide fields
Where War its baton of destruction wields—
Where nations stake existence on a blow,
And lives are played with, like the dicer's throw.
Here, in a narrow room, with cold, bare walls,
Where the reflected daylight faintly falls,—
Where comfort long has been a mocking name
And bare existence feebly makes its claim,—
Here toils humanity in noblest guise,
To those who see with labour's earnest eyes.
It is the inventor's chamber : scattered wide
Before, around, and thick on every side,
Are dusty wheels and pulleys, straps and screws,
That few can name and fewer yet can use.
Tools stud the beams, whose use we guess in vain,
And diagrams adorn the dusky pane.

c

Here, in the centre, stands a silent mass—
Iron, and leather, copper, wood and brass,
All mixed and mingled in mechanic shapes—
Retorts, and cranks, and pulleys, and escapes;
A thought in skeleton—a morning dream
Got up in metal shape for air or steam ;
Something to bless the world, when quite evolved,
With truths elicited and problems solved,—
To show the human mind in form expressed,
And give to labour's weary muscles rest;—
Or something—who shall say ?—to prove at last
An *ignis fatuus* troublesome and vast,—
One costly, long and difficult mistake
O'er which the world shall scoff and hearts shall break.

XIX.

But wheels are silent—pinions fail to turn ;
Springs, straps nor pulleys share the mind's concern :
All dumb—all senseless, save one throbbing brain
That labours on, though labour be but vain.
Beside his work the inventor sits—his eye
Scanning some point his busy hand must try ;
His thin face peering through the dusty maze,
Stamped with his sleepless nights and weary days ;
His face attenuated, cold and thin,
Tough bones and muscles ridging through the skin ;
Gray pent-house brows o'er which the forehead pales,
And long stiff hair that lies in frosty swales ;

Bent at the shoulders—shrunken at the hips—
His thread-bare clothing in a sad eclipse ;
All the lost pride that man could need to lose
Shown in the slouching of his stringless shoes ;
His thin hands working with unsteady haste,
As if he felt the moments run to waste :
Here sits th'inventor—type of all his kind
Who rashly leave the sluggish age behind.

XX.

Can man be poorer ?—man our pity share
More strongly than the bent form hovering there ?
Ah ! little knows the mind that dares the thought,
That subtle pride with every soul inwrought !
What though amid his tangled rods and wheels
His brain grows dizzy and his reason reels ?—
What though for days—for months—for weary years
Down a long lane of toil success appears ?—
What though he *has* been cold, and faint, and weak,
And hunger thins the life-blood in his cheek ?—
What though e'en now, ere those dull pinions start,
The wheels of life are clogging in his heart ?—
Is not his great work here—his hope—his pride ?—
His friend—his sister—daughter—ay ! his bride !
Bride to whose sluggish heart his pulses move
With something fonder than a husband's love ?
Has he not *made* it ? Is't not trebly great
To feel that power can fashion and create ?

And when 'tis done—ay, *when 'tis done*—how earth
Shall bless that long and painful iron birth!
'Tis *almost* done: one little blemish here,
And there another, yet awhile appear,
But what are *they?* spots on a noonday sun!
Mere nothings, in a triumph almost won!

XXI.

" Yes! yes! I see it!" speaks the tongue restrained,
As some new insight through the mass is gained:
" I see it all! one touch—but one touch more,
And where *I* stand man never stood before!
Rich—envied—honoured— all my glory won;—
I see the daylight—it is *almost* done!"
He rises, with a gesture weak and wild,
Stretches his arms to clasp his spirit child;
Totters above it; then the hunger pain
Gnaws through the heart and stupefies the brain:
One short, quick gasp, and there, with closing eyes,
Beside the labour of his life he lies.
Almost the dull wheels moved—they do no more:
Their life, with his, lies ebbing on the floor.
That hidden power, by one slight error chained,
Must still remain unknown and unattained!
Almost completed—useless now, and lost—
Ha! sure some figure o'er the threshold crossed,
Some hand lifts up the fallen man, and plies
A cordial draught, unsealing lips and eyes.

He lives! His great work yet full fame may shed
Through years of glory on his silvered head:
Almost successful, and BUT *almost* dead!

XXII.

Again the evening woos us to its breast
With shadowy promises of peace and rest—
With glimpses from that realm of hope and pride
That none may force, yet none may be denied—
The realm where human love's sweet tendrils cling,
Where human love's fresh fountains gush and spring,
Where lingers all of Eden ever known,
And no man walks, or thinks, or breathes alone.
The sun slants low the shadows o'er the mead;
The piled clouds glow like domes of kingly deed;
The breeze is softened to a whispering air
Just formed to bear a kiss or nurse a prayer;
And earth appears an infant's hush to keep
Ere night, the soother, cradles her to sleep.
A broad piazza overlooks the vale,
Dotting far off the green with presence pale.
Behind it, half in white, and half in green,
A home of country competence is seen;—
Half white, where paint has drawn its cool, pale lines;
Half green, beneath its load of clinging vines.

XXIII.

But two there are on those piazza seats
For whom the eye forgets all else it meets:
Two girls—and both are young, and both are fair,
Both spotless as the snowy robes they wear;
But one has eyes of blue, and hair of gold,—
One eyes of black, and hair of raven fold,
And well they seem for artist contrast placed,—
Head bent to head and arms encircling waist.
But one—and she it is with golden curls,
The gentlest, softest, fairest of the girls,—
Bends down her eyes as if with very shame,
While both the other's mirth and mischief flame.
A heart untouched beams through those keen dark eyes,
While in the blue, love's faint, dim shadow lies.
" You hear his horse's hoof, sly girl, I know!"
And redder seem the hearer's cheeks to glow.
" You hear him coming! fie! what love and pride!
But one hour more, and you will be a bride!"
" Hush!" and the reddening face finds hidden rest
In the white folds that veil the other's breast—
" Hush!" and so soft she lies, with pleading will,
The red lips kiss her forehead, then are still;
But the low words *she* utters flow along
Softer than ripples—sweeter far than song:
" I thought I heard him coming—yes, 'twas true;
And then a feeling strange, and sweet, and new,

' *Almost a bride* '—came with his love endeared ;
I was so happy that I almost *feared!* "
" Feared, little trembler ? " but no more is heard :
The sleeping echoes by a sound are stirred—
A cry that seems to speak some mortal throe
Comes ringing from the road a mile below,
And on the instant, breaking into sight,
His horse comes, riderless, in headlong flight,

XXIV.

Almost a bride—Oh, maid with golden hair,
Pray, if the heart has strength enough for prayer ;
For bruised and mangled from the flinty road
They bear him to that desolate abode.
Life flickers in his pulses, faint and low ;
His thick breath heaves with long, convulsive throe ;
The bloody foam between his set teeth creeps,
And o'er his glazing eye the sternest weeps.
Her white dress stained with blood, beside his bed
Kneels, crazed with grief, she of the sunny head,
Kisses the chilling lips, the stiffening hand,
Holding her tears at terrible command,—
And as the old clock tolls with cruel might
The midnight moment of her bridal night—
Sees the last change come o'er the staring eye—
Sees lover—husband—heave one breath, and *die !*
Almost a bride—almost, but never more—
She bears all grief that ever woman bore ;

Bears it, till comes that heavier, bitterer blow
Which lays a second time her idol low,—
Bears it, till through her broken sobs she learns
How worthless was the life her memory urns—
Already wedded—stained with every crime,
And mercifully dead in Heaven's good time!
Almost a bride—see fate bridge o'er the void,
And save the victim when *almost* destroyed.

XXV.

The key-note Crime is sounded—let the view
Dwell on its varying phases, ever new,
And mark—with virtue sharing human force—
How fall the same restrictions in its course.
A hall of old comes glimmering on the sight—
A hall with luxury rich, with beauty bright.
Silks from all zones, and velvets deeply piled;—
Woods on whose fragrance tropic suns have smiled;—
Vessels of crystal and of ruddy gold
That maddening draughts from dusky cellars hold;—
These, under arches fretted, proud and high,
And ceilings flushed with starlight, like a sky,—
These well befit the revellers fair and proud
Who round the board in gay disorder crowd.
Velvets and satins crusted o'er with gems;—
Laces that frost the silken garment-hems,
Each cobwebbed mesh a thing of costly pride
That best displays the charms it seems to hide,—

All pale before the shapes that round us rise, ⎤
Tall forms, and rounded limbs, and flashing eyes — ⎬
A nation's noblest, in their merriest guise. ⎦

XXVI.

The dance goes twining in a mystic chain,
Bewildering thought —o'erheating blood and brain,—
To sounds that from the balcony on high
Seem dropping, liquid, from some tropic sky.
Cheeks glow, and bosoms flush, and soft hands press
In passion's wild, bewildering caress;
And chains are weaving, powerful as light,
Shall make all life a very bloom or blight.
But two there are—fit theme for tale or song—
Two on whose forms the vision lingers long;—
Two, on whose faces beauty, wealth and birth
Have set the triple charms that fetter earth.
One manly, with his form of glorious mould,
Lip, cheek and forehead stern, but never cold;
One womanly, as woman might have been
Ere Eden gloomed upon the primal sin.
And they are each the other's: lip to ear
Seems ever whispering words but one should hear;
And one moves not, but in the other's eyes
A wish to follow sweetly seems to rise.
On love's wild stream, beyond all line or lure,
They float towards each other, fast and sure.

Almost their love, if good or ill its power,
Has burst from budding bloom to fruit and flower.

XXVII.

Almost : but one, with sternly flashing eye,
Has held the lovers as they circled by,
And in the shadow some have marked him stand,
With lip compressed and fiercely gripping hand ;
Yet none have wondered—none perchance have thought
What evil passion on his features wrought.
Anon a change comes o'er him—from his face
The clouds have passed and left no outward trace ;
And none could dream of either guilt or guile
Beneath the calm deception of his smile.
The dancers pause, and, gliding towards the board
With every wine and every viand stored,—
Upon the lover's arm he lays his hand
And says—in tone half plea and half command :
" One draught with me—we have not drank to-night,
And wines may flash, though beauty's eyes be bright."
He brims two goblets, but with fingers skilled
Drops into one a powder ere 'tis filled.
None see the motion, for the lover's gaze
Across the hall one fatal moment strays,
And all beside have eyes and ears alone
For loves or hates that measure with their own.
He lifts the poisoned flask, and bowing low
Gives to the victim love has made his foe.

The lover takes, and raises to his lip—
God! if one draught—one drop he blindly sip,
Within an hour death's pang his spirit rives,
For in it lies the bane of twenty lives.

XXVIII.

See! his white fingers clasp the goblet stem;
His red lips touch its edge of gold and gem;
He breathes th' aroma of th' immortal fields,
That ripe old wine before its poison yields;
Almost he sips his death: a moment more,
And through his veins the fatal tide shall pour,
As, lipping the unpoisoned cup meanwhile,
The murderer rays out his deadly smile.
Life hangs upon a breath, when—hark! a cry,
A sound that may be moan, or shriek or sigh,—
A cry from woman's lip, and then a pause,
As all press forward to discern the cause.
Both join the crowd that toward the door have poured;
Both goblets drop untasted on the board,
But one—the one which holds that fatal pledge
Is set too near for safety to the edge,
And as he passes by, a careful guest
Changes its due position to the rest.
'Tis but a woman fainting from the heat,
And with a " Pshaw! " the crowd relieved retreat.
He whose swift work of death is almost done—
Whose love and vengeance both are nearly won,—

Cannot endure one hour his project crossed,
His opportunity so cheaply lost.
"The sparkles yet o'erkiss the rosy tide,
Nor strength nor flavour in the wine have died.
If yet we loiter all the gems will sink,"
He says, and hands the goblet—"let us drink!"

XXIX.

No interruption now, for hate and crime
Will find their opportunity and time.
They drink: the red wine overflows the edge,
Kisses the lips just silent from the pledge,
And thrills the blood through every circling vein
With a new feeling blent of joy and pain.
The deed is done! the deed? but is it told?
Whose lip and brow grow rigid, dead and cold?
Who falls, when hearts with fear and horror freeze,
And terror-shaken smite the trembling knees?
The lover stands unharmed, though blanched his
    cheek,
And by him droops the lady, pale and weak;
But he who mixed the potion foul and rank
Himself at last the ruin sipped and drank,
And dead 'neath flashing lights and staring eyes
A ghastly monument of hate he lies.
The goblets in that moment's pause were changed;
The poisoner is on himself avenged!

Almost triumphant in the Borgia's guilt ;
Almost a nobler life in malice spilt ;
Then sent to fill the tomb himself has built.

XXX.

Still turn the glass. For ceilings flushed with
    gold,
Here have we mouldy rafters, bare and old ;
For silken hangings from the Indian looms,
And lights, and gems, and music, and perfumes,—
Here have we bare, discolored, grimy walls
And light that through the broken casement
    crawls,
And smells that come from fever and from want
When human life is drying at the font.
Starvation holds a dread pre-emption here,
And misery has a title doubly clear.
Beside the cheap pine table—head on hand,
One poor dip candle by her on its stand,
With garments thin, but sadly thinner face
Where lingers yet some long-lost girlish grace,—
A woman sits—a woman, if that name
The lost and hopeless of her sex may claim.
No food upon the bare and empty shelf,
Unless that half-starved mouse might eat himself ;
No ember in the fire-place, though the air
Bites with the chill of winter and despair.

XXXI.

Her thin lips move : she mutters broken words
With voice that once had shamed the evening
  birds,—
So dissonant and harsh, and feeble now,—
'Twere mockery could it name a lover's vow ;
Yet lover's vow lips spoke and ears received,
Or she, poor fool! had been but half bereaved.
"'Tis *almost* done!" she says, with moaning speech—
" There is but one step more of crime to reach!
My father, with his honored silver hairs,
From me met death in answer to his prayers ;
My soul I murdered—murdered long ago,
In guilt's caress and wine's delirious flow ;
There but remains one horror strange and new—
The body left me I must murder, too!
Cold, hunger, beating, curses, I have borne,
My heart by each corroded, gnawed and worn ;
The last poor crust, a spaniel's need beneath,
I ground this morning 'tween my gnashing teeth ;
To-day I saw the last faint spark expire
Of that poor solace of the naked—fire.
'Tis *almost* done—my penance, with my sin:
Let the dread tortures of the lost begin ! "
She rises feebly, though she scarce can stand,
Into her bosom thrusts her trembling hand ;
Quick-flitting agonies o'er her features pass
As forth she draws a little globe of glass.

" I am not fit to live, then what have I
For refuge, but the last resource, to die !
They say self-murder's tortures never cease :
No matter, so it brings me present peace ! "
'Tis *almost over :* from the vial's jaws
The last obstruction her weak hand withdraws ;
One poison drop will cool her life-long drouth
She thinks, and slowly raises to her mouth.
Oh, fatal deed, though long and sorely tried !
Almost a starveling and a suicide !

XXXII.

The poor have little need of bolt or bar
The burglar's plan of robbery to mar ;
And joy for her, o'erhanging ruin's brink,
That one can enter ere she dares to drink.
No knock is heard upon the broken door,
No footstep sounds upon the naked floor.
Yet close behind her steals a human form,
Eyes smile upon her, pitiful and warm ;
A quick grasp on her wrist—a shrieked surprise—
And shattered on the hearth the vial lies.
She turns—beside her sees an angel stand,
A *human* angel, life within her hand,—
Falls on her knees, and sobs, and weeps, and prays,
With all the fervour of her better days.
One moment by the Tempter fast enslaved—
Almost destroyed—then fed, and clothed, and saved.

XXXIII.

Here sits the slave of wealth—the man whose mind
Through half a century keeps one god enshrined,—
One yellow god, with graven, glittering face,
Who holds, as vassals, half the human race.
His god is gold—his heaven, that coming hour
When he shall hold within his single power
Enough of wealth to fill one hungry soul:
Oh, desert track, a mirage for the goal!
But now 'tis almost ended, for at last
He holds enough of ruddy gold amassed—
Enough of house, and land, and bill, and bond,
To leave small margin worth his thought, beyond.
Small margin? yes, there *is* a margin still,—
A little corner of the heart to fill,
And then his golden happiness is sure;
That makes him rich—its want still leaves him poor.
" *Almost* enough!" he says, with sleepy yawn,
As the last balance-sheet is deftly drawn:
" Almost enough—one year of struggle more,
Then Fortune may close up her golden door!
All won—none lost—no needless fraction spent—
Twelve months of gain, and I shall be content!"

XXXIV.

At midnight clash the bells, and all the air
Is thick with smoke, and spark, and lurid glare.

Walls topple—engines clash—and hydrants flow,
And ruined men rush useless to and fro.
The fire eats through the city's very heart;
It desolates the great commercial mart;
It sweeps the spot where heaviest rental lies;
On every fiery wing a fortune flies.
Ere morning, blackened bricks and smoking stones
Are all the wealth the ruined merchant owns.
One little wreck of all those glorious shapes—
His cloud-piled domes of fortune—still escapes;
Enough to nerve him on his toil anew
O'er that long wilderness once wandered through;
Enough—and nothing more—his heart to bear
Above starvation and a death-despair.
Almost the wide world's wonder of success;
Then famed for loss and ruin not the less.

XXXV.

Here, by a table strewn with census-books,
And lists and rolls that fright us with their looks,—
With papers filling every vacant chair,
And documents in cubes of ponderous square,—
The politician sits. An earnest man
Who thinks that time with politics began,
And quick could tell, to serve some party good,
How ended every ballot since the flood.
He plays with destiny, and chance, and fate,
Crazed with the noisy welfare of the State;

D

All sounds discordant, save from patriot throats,
And figures only good for counting votes.
A life-long struggle his for power and place,
Fought on through years of failure and disgrace ;
The time still coming, when the people's voice
Shall crown him with the glory of their choice.
And now the race is ending. South and North,
East, West—all sections pour their plaudits forth ;
Figures—those stubborn things which never lie,
Have shown the very turning of the die ;
Another hour, and victory's loud acclaim
Shall flout the heavens with one triumphant name,
And nought remain except the pleasant toil
Of gathering up and portioning the spoil.
Almost elected: one more count he waits,
To mock at chance, and dare the very fates !
The messenger is coming—give him wings
To speed the news of victory that he brings !

XXXVI.

The messenger is here: he questions why
That lingering step—that dull and troubled eye ?
Do figures falsify at last ? not so,
But estimates are high, and facts are low ;
The gold of bribery perchance has missed,
Or taken strength that right could ill resist ;
One thoughtless word a deadly foe has made,
Or some old foible been anew displayed ;

It matters little what the check we meet,
If over it we stumble to defeat.
Some other ear must catch the plaudit cries;
Some other hand must portion out the prize.
Almost elected—ah! the bitter tear
Drops hotter, failing with the end so near.
Another tear in gratitude may fall
When after years have filled and ripened all;
When he who trod so near the dizzy height
Sees all the issue in a clearer light,—
Learns how the brightest fame grows soiled and dark;
Exposed to envious jest and foul remark,—
Learns how success may mar and failure make;
A grand achievement oft a grand mistake.
When this shall come, the politician's eye
The truth of human life may yet espy,
Almost elected keep its charm no more
And *almost ruined* take the place it bore!

XXXVII.

Here stands a prisoner, with guilty hands,
Whose life the creed of " blood for blood " demands;
Bench, bar and jury mustering strength and skill
To vindicate the law—" Thou shalt not kill! "
But still no eye beheld the deed of blood
When the armed hand let out the crimson flood,
And only circumstance, that distance dims,
Can draw the fetter round the guilty limbs.

Some links are wanting in the chain of proof;
Some threads are lacking in the legal woof;
One failure more, and all the rest will fail,
Nor gallows swing for him, nor open jail.
Almost he stands acquitted of his crime
And ready for the guilt of after-time.
Almost :—but something more may yet be done
To free him from the web the law has spun,—
To clear that foul suspicion from his head
And smooth the brows that speak their shuddering
    dread.
It must be done : he towards his counsel leans,
Whispers the subtle question that he means ;
The counsel to the witness on the stand
Quick puts it, at his client's brief command ;
That question all the missing link supplies,
The thick woof gathers, and the murderer dies !
Almost escaped : then, by his own blind deed,
Sent to his punishment with headlong speed.

XXXVIII.

A month goes by, and in those very walls
Where on the guilty swift destruction falls,—
An innocent man stands pleading with the law,
But vainly as the drowning grasps his straw.
Close wedged around him stand the stubborn facts,
Admissions, contradictions, looks and acts.
He *must* be guilty !—says the public cry :

He *must* be guilty!—he is doomed to die.
Almost his dim hope dwindles to a speck ;
Almost he feels the rough rope press his neck,—
When, shaken by the voices deep and loud,
The corniced ceiling falls amid the crowd.
A dozen men are injured by the fall,
But one sharp shriek of pain rings over all.
One victim, by the fragments crushed and maimed,
Before an hour the victor death has claimed ;
And in his pangs he mutters faint and low
That *his* hand struck the black and guilty blow !
The clouds roll off, that dimmed the other's fame,
And yet how near a felon's death he came !
Almost a victim to the law's mistakes ;
Then saved and honoured, as the mystery breaks.

XXXIX.

And here a drunkard staggers towards his end,
Incarnate drink his last remaining friend ;
Hope, fortune, life, all sunken in the bowl,
And phantom demons playing for his soul.
Almost the human shape has left his face
And the brute beast usurped its sacred place ;
Almost he totters down that dark abyss
Where through crazed brains ghosts haunt and serpents
        hiss ;
Almost he knows, at life's eternal cost,
What horrors fill that word of mourning—lost !

Almost : thank God that yet such things may be
As stumbling feet once more from stumbling free !
Some word of counsel lights his darkened mind—
Shows him the doom before—the wreck behind ;
And fed and clothed, a sober man once more,
He shows—what seemed a doubtful thing before,—
That hope's dim lamp *may* burn till life is o'er.
Almost destroyed : heaven teach where safety lies !
E'en slight indulgence will not win the prize
And its best hope in sure temptation dies.

XL.

There is another boundary—hard to name ;
A risk more terrible than life or fame.
Two champions—Good and Ill—a soul their stake,
Through the long centuries their lances break,—
Almost a spirit lost—a spirit won ;
And earth will shrivel ere the fight is done.
There may be phantoms fierce and shadows pale
To fright the hand would stretch within the Veil ;
And lightning bolts may play around his head
Who in the shadow of the Throne would tread.
And yet—the word be breathed with reverent awe,
As those should breathe who near the Presence draw,—
And yet—the Eternal Hills are hard to climb,
Clothed in the frosts of earth—the mists of time.
Thick warning marks are set along the way,
Yet some misread, and many go astray ;

And in the silent night sometimes we hear
A sound that strikes us with a shuddering fear,—
A sound as if some spirit mounting high,
Scaling the peaks that pierce the upper sky,—
Had lost its footing on the verge of bliss,
Hovered a moment o'er the black abyss,
Then downward—downward—like some toppled stone,
Sunk where no ray of light has ever shone.

XLI.

There may be those on whom the Spirit's light
Has glanced like morning sunbeams, warm and bright,
Thawing away the crust of rock and ice,
Changing the feet from wrong, the wish from vice ;—
There may be those to whom the spirit gives
A throb of gladness that th' Eternal lives,—
Who feel some drawing of the marriage bond
That links our nature to the God beyond ;—
There may be those who upward reach their palms,
Asking for good, as beggars plead for alms,—
Who struggle onward, toil, and faint, and wait,
And see the Mountains and the Golden Gate,
Almost among the number dim revealed—
The twelve times twelve of thousands set and scaled ;—
There may be those—woe worth some darling sin !—
Who see the goal, and touch, but never win !
Almost a Christian—said the heathen king
With whose remembered words this thought took wing :

Be ours, oh bounteous Heaven, as here our theme
Fades to the dim proportions of a dream,—
Be ours, oh bounteous Heaven, the better way !
And light our footsteps with that purer ray
Whose *Almost* brightens into perfect day !

II.

RHYMES OF LIFE AND OCCASION.

BEHIND THE ORGAN.

In the golden Sabbath morning, when the sunshine filled
the street,
And the pleasure-seekers hurried by with quick and
eager feet,—
Ere the bells clashed out their summons to the house of
praise and prayer,—
Through the old church door I entered—gray old church
across the square.

Quaint and old the gray-haired sexton, with his massive
iron key;
Quaint and old the house his kindness many a time
unlocked to me:
Quainter—older far than both, the volumes I had handled
oft,—
Sleeping in the antique book-case, in the dusty organ-
loft.

Fénélon, Bossuet and Butler—Taylor of the silver
    tongue,—
Old Jerome and Athanasius—lamps above time's mid-
    night hung,—
Cotton Mather—Roger Williams—Tennent, of the holy
    trance,—
All together, oddly jumbled, met the student's anxious
    glance.

Proud was he—the gray old sexton—of the treasures in
    his trust—
Proud of every centuried volume—of their lore and of
    their dust;
And the key he gave me often trembled with the sudden
    thought—
What if harm to oak or parchment should some reckless
    day be wrought?

But the key was never wanting, for I bore a mightier
    still—
Earnest youth in reverence pleading to old age's
    kindly will;
And mayhap the sexton's musing took this fond, romantic
    tone:
That the visits might be welcome, as the old saints lived
    alone.

Down before the oaken book-case low I sat me on the
floor,
Piling round me heavy volumes of devotion's love and
lore ;—
Sipping one and then another of those olden hearts
profound,
Till, a very bee polemic, in the golden wealth I drowned.

Floating through my drowsy brain I heard St. Simeon
Stylites
Preaching on his penance pillar, in the pain that brought
him ease ;—
Heard the sackcloth priests denouncing pride and wealth,
in accents bold,—
Heard the chants that through the arches o'er the
gathered Councils rolled.

Floating through my drowsy brain I heard the city's
quiet hum,
Blended with the Convenauter's preaching on his pulpit-
drum ;—
Heard some martyr shout exultant as the flames around
him played ;—
Followed on with mad old Peter, as he preached the
First Crusade.

Then the sounds grew faint and distant, and the type,
    so fair and large—
Taylor's holy "Preparation" to the nobles of his
    charge—
Grew at last a fading glimmer ; then no more the line I
    kept,
And with head on old Chrysostom on the floor I sank
    and slept.

Hark ! what sounds were those that woke me ?—sounds
    that smote the shuddering air
Till the senses in their labyrinth sunk in quiet, lost
    despair ?—
Sounds that overcame my being, like some blinding,
    rushing tide,
Bearing me upon its bosom, till I struggled, sank and
    died !

Shrill and loud I heard the shrieks that might have filled
    the upper deep
When the Minions of the Shadow took their last eternal
    leap :
Deep and low I heard the thunders, crashing through
    the vault of heaven—
As the wrath of the Eternal, falling on the Unfor-
    given.

Reason drowned, and sense lay gasping: I but heard
    the torrent sweep:
If I slept, what phantom voices chased each other
    through my sleep!
Then they blended—then they mingled—and a swooning
    child I lay
On the sea of sound and fancy floating helplessly away

Nuns were chanting in the chapels—friars' voices
    blending hoarse;
Then broke in the Haarlem organ, with its wild and
    thundering force;
Then the Minnesingers chanted knightly deed and
    ladies' praise,
When the Feast of Harps was given, in the Wartburg's
    golden days.

Crashed the thunder—mighty armies battered down
    the walls of doom:
Wailed the dirge—some noble heart went sadly to its
    honoured tomb:
Sounded lute—I heard the whispers in the ears of
    noble dames:
Clashed the bell—I heard the thousands battling with
    destruction's flames.

Then a dirge the great sea sang me, and a wail the
    mountain pines ;
And I heard the low wind moaning round old History's
    broken shrines :
Then the Norseman sang his death-song, seated on his
    barrow-mound,
And the Indian shouted gaily o'er his happy hunting-
    ground.

Then the spell grew deeper—deeper : louder, higher
    swelled the peal
And I felt my struggling senses—dizzy senses—faint
    and reel :
All the world—all time—all heaven—filled the chorus
    loud and long,—
Time's farewell and heaven's beginning—the climacteric
    of song.

Then I knew that I was listening—I, so helpless and
    forlorn—
To the General Assembly and the Church of the First-
    Born—
To the Twelve Times Twelve of Thousands—all whose
    names are writ in heaven,—
To the anthem of the Perfect—to the song of the
    Forgiven.

Sought my tongue to join the chorus, but my lips no
  utterance gave ;
I could drown but could not float in all that dense
  melodic wave !
On my brow the thick beads started : I was struggling
  for my breath
I was fighting with the phantom of the great Eternal
  Death !

Silence ! Peace ! a human footstep broke at last the
  subtle charm,
And the gray-haired sexton's hand was kindly laid upon
  my arm :
Head against the organ-casing I had slept the service
  through :
What would buy the long emotions that Behind the
  Organ grew ?

JOHN CHINAMAN.

JOHN CHINAMAN deals in Havana cigars—
 Those wondrous Havanas of mullein and oak
Not often vouchsafed to terrestrial bars,
 And that need a steam-engine to light and to smoke.
John Chinaman fills up his fumigant stock
 With those splendid and costly Manilla cheroots,
One whiff of which perfumes the whole of a block,
 And one puff of which pulls a man out of his boots.

John Chinaman sells to you " Solace " and " Gem,"
 " John Anderson," "Lilienthal," " Cornish," and Co. ;
And he keeps a few pipes with diminutive stem,
 Some matches for lights, and a " Smoker " or so.
Tobacco—John " sabés " of nothing beyond :
 He thrives not in brushes, or tooth-picks, or combs :
And we wonder if Chinaland, over the pond,
 Has nicotine pap in its crockery homes ?

John Chinaman floated, there can't be a doubt,
 Down some Yang-Tse-Ki-ang-Tse of river, to sea ;
And still he keeps floating and floating about—
 A condemned and thrown-overboard chest of green
  tea.
On nothing he sees look his little pig eyes ;—
 They are gazing with quiet and patient despair
Towards that Flowery Land that the circle supplies,
 While the whole of the world is the rest of the
  square.

John Chinaman sits at the old Park gate—
 That gate which is useless for want of a fence ;
With the stoical calm of a saint or a fate
 He sells his tobacco and gathers his cents.
Be it sunshine or storm, it is nothing to John—
 Cold nor sunshine can harm that rhinoceros hide :
If you miss him some day, you may know he is gone
 Where the rats are not roasted, nor kittens are fried.

John Chinaman—type of a far-away race—
 With your fancy for pig-tail (tobacco or hair)—
I think I can trace on your dusky old face
 The marks of disease, and of age, and of care,
Will you leave us some day, John ? and if this should
 be,
 Have you dear *little* Chinamen, dirty and squat,
All ready to share, in this land of the free,
 The kicks and the coppers that fall to your lot ?

If with you, John, the race has a chance to run out,
  Pray, before you go hence with your awning and
    box—
Do solve me, dear John, this most horrible doubt
  That so often my faith in humanity shocks :
That cigar you are smoking—oh, is it the same
  As the bundle you offer ? or, deaf to our groans,
Have you learned from the butchers that civilized
    game—
  To eat all the meat and sell off all the bones ?

John Chinaman—type of a far-away race—
  Little ant of the Orient, dusky and brown—
God forbid I should sneer at that weather-worn face,
  Or begrudge you your corner, in country or town !
Your place will be vacant, but so will be mine !
  Caucasian—Mongolian—there's little to choose :
And the world will not care, when we're over the line,
  Whether puppies or oysters have furnished our stews.

New York, 1860.

THE SHADOW AT THE KEYS.

"I played the 'Last Rose of Summer' the last thing before I came
away, and left the piano full of it. If you want to hear it at any
time, you have only to set up my chair and open the instrument.
I will be there to play for you."—[*A word at parting*].

THE absent fingers touch no more the keys ;
  The music in them lies as dead and cold
As some great statue of Praxiteles
  In the unchiselled marble lay of old.
The sweet face that o'erbent them with a smile—
  The soft, warm lips faint echoing every tone—
In the dark void of absence rest awhile,
  And almost seem to leave us each alone.

Midnight and silence ! Let me try the charm
  Soft spoken through a mist of smiles and tears !—
Try wizard spells that have no power to harm,
  And people air without the sorcerer's fears !
Set up the chair that held her rounded form ;
  With reverential care unlock the case ;
See the white keys where slept her fingers warm—
  Then start and shudder at the vacant place !

Vacant? Not so! Is't fancy? Do I dream?—
 Through the thin air a soft, dim outline shows;
I see dark hair down dimpled shoulders stream;
 A girlish face from out the shadow grows.
The rosy fingers into semblance start,
 And flicker o'er the ivory, doubly white:
Remoulded by the magic of the heart,
 She sits before me—gentle, warm and bright!

But oh, so silent! Does the omen fail
 When half accomplished? List, with hushing breath!
Through the still keys there creeps a plaintive wail,
 Too sad for joy, and yet too sweet for death.
It rises like the wind-harp—sinks and dies—
 Rises again and lingers on the ear,
Till the Last Rose its helpless sorrow sighs,
 And its spent dew-drops gather in a tear.

It is the olden touch—I know it well,
 But mortal touch ne'er moulded sounds like these:
Woven in fancy—fashioned by a spell—
 It is not played but dreamed upon the keys!
From all the realms of poesy and song—
 From the pure heaven whose harps it may have
  kissed—
There seems a tenderer pathos borne along,
 That dims the eye-sight with a loving mist.

Tears fall—the throat chokes up with silent speech,
  And the pained heart with sad emotion throbs,
As o'er the keys the phantom fingers reach
  And the low music wastes in broken sobs.
It might be wailing o'er some new-made grave
  Where yet life's memory lives on brow and breast;
Or moaning where the grasses nod and wave
  Above some early love's forgotten rest.

No more! I cannot bear it! Break the charm!
  One longer, deeper wail:—the keys are still!
I see the fading of a fair white arm—
  A face dissolves like mist upon a hill.
I am alone, dear daughter!—all alone
  With midnight, silence, and the yearning fear
Which clusters ever round a love unknown
  And makes the loved in absence doubly dear.

1861.

HEARTS OF OAK AND STONE.

Gray rock on the rough and rugged shore—
   By the wild southeaster bruised and beaten,—
For ever dinned by the sullen roar,
   By Time's fierce tooth defaced and eaten,—
Thick set on thy scarred and mangled brow
   The scourging marks of a thousand Winters,
And bearing the track of the spoiler's plough
   In thy yawning seams and jagged splinters!

There's a secret in thy stony heart—
   A secret hidden away for ages—
That I would wring, with a cruel art,
   To be written and read on human pages:
Is there not, beneath that icy chill,
   Some struggling pulse that the mind may measure?—
Some spark from God's own mind and will,
   That may writhe in pain and thrill in pleasure?

Art thou never a-cold, thou gray old stone,
  In the Arctic blasts of the bleak December,
When the cold creeps in to the blood and bone,
  And penury sobs o'er its dying ember?
Art thou never lonely, and sad, and dread—
  All night in the desolate darkness lying,—
With a starless sky, as if heaven were dead,
  And the storm-clouds black like spectres flying?

Dost thou never shrink, when the fiend unlocks
  The gates of the east wind wild and frantic,
And the terrible gales of the equinox
  Come sweeping in o'er the vexed Atlantic?—
When the angry surge breaks wild and high,
  A fury of foam over beaches and ledges,
And the maddened waves, as they hurry by,
  Strike cruel and fierce as the Titan sledges?

Dost thou never warm in the sun of May,
  When heaven is aglow and earth is laughing,
Till the tingling thrills through thy dull veins play,
  As ours when the lips old wine are quaffing?
Dull stone!—sad stone!—no answer falls,
  Through those iron lips, to our human wonder;
And none will be heard till the trumpet calls,
  And the rocks and the mountains shiver asunder.

Rough oak, with the gnarled and tangled limbs,
    On the crest of the storm-lashed mountain-ridges,—
Where the cloud through thy branches heavenward
      swims,
    And the peaks seem piers of aërial bridges ;—
With boughs all twisted, and rent, and torn,
    Where in springs of old the song-birds nestled,—
With bark all scaled, and shriveled, and worn,
    By the gales thy giant-arms have wrestled ;—

Hast thou no voice, oh heart of oak ?—
    No answer the waiting ear to proffer,—
Of what, since the clouds thy coming broke,
    It has been thy lot to joy and to suffer ?—
Of the wind of ice and snow, that came
    And twisted away thy topmost branches ?—
Of the levin bolt, whose angry flame
    At thy body the sultry August launches ?

When falls the pelting and pitiless rain,
    And high on the ridge thou'rt swaying and rocking,—
When the lights are gone from the villager's pane,
    And the shrieks of the blast seem demons mocking,—
When thy stoutest branches murmur and creak,
    And their toughest fibres seem failing and rotten,—
Has thy heart no despair, the thought to speak,
    That thy Maker the work of His hands has forgotten ?

Does the snow of the Winter ne'er chill thy root?
   Does the owl never fright thee with horrible raving?
Dost thou envy no tree its golden fruit?
   Nor feel the Spring breath that the world is laving?
Is the tale of the Dryads false and vain—
   The brain-sick dream of a weak romancer?
Old oak of the mountains, loose the chain
   That binds thee in silence, and hear, and answer!

All dumb—all silent! Rock and Tree
   Keep hidden the secret by Heaven confided!
'Tis enough, oh dreamer!—enough for thee
   To be sure of the Hand that formed and guided.
Let the ear lie close to old Nature's breast;
   Ban the credulous fool, and contemn the despiser;
Then wait, with a spirit calm and at rest,
   For the lore of the ages better and wiser!

THE CHILDREN IN THE WOOD.

Tell us—poor gray-haired children that we are—
Tell us some story of the days afar,
Down shining through the years like sun and star.

The stories that when we were very young,
Like golden beads on lips of wisdom hung,
At fireside told or by the cradle sung.

Not Cinderella with the tiny shoe,
Nor Hassan's carpet that through distance flew,
Nor Jack the Giant-Killer's derring-do.

Not even the little lady of the Hood;
But something sadder—easier understood—
The ballad of the Children in the Wood.

Poor babes! the cruel uncle lives again,
To whom their little voices plead in vain—
Who sent them forth to be by ruffians slain.

The hapless agent of the guilt is here—
From whose seared heart their pleading brought a tear—
Who could not strike, but fled away in fear.

And hand in hand the wanderers, left alone,
Through the dense forest make their feeble moan,
Fed on the berries—pillowed on a stone.

Still hand in hand, till little feet grow sore,
And fails the feeble strength their limbs that bore ;
Then they lie down, and feel the pangs no more.

The stars shine down in pity from the sky ;
The night-bird marks their fate with plaintive cry ;
The dew-drop wets their parched lips ere they die.

There clasped they lie—death's poor, unripened sheaves—
Till the red robin through the tree-top grieves,
And flutters down and covers them with leaves.

'Tis an old legend, and a touching one :
What then ? Methinks beneath to-morrow's sun
Some deed as heartless will be planned and done.

Children of older years and sadder fate
Will wander, outcasts, from the great world's gate,
And ne'er return again, though long they wait.

Through wildering labyrinths that round them close,
In that heart-hunger disappointment knows,
They long may wander ere the night's repose.

Their feeble voices through the dusk may call,
And on the ears of busy mortals fall ;
But who will hear, save God above us all ?

Will wolfish Hates forego their evil work,
Nor Envy's vultures in the branches perk,
Nor Slander's snakes within the verdure lurk ?

And when at last the torch of life grows dim,
Shall sweet birds o'er them chant a burial hymn,
Or decent pity veil the stiffening limb ?

Thrice happy they, if the old legend stand,
And they are left to wander hand in hand—
Not driven apart by Eden's blazing brand !

If, long before the lonely night comes on—
By tempting berries wildered and withdrawn—
One does not look and find the other gone ;—

If something more of shame, and grief, and wrong
Than that so often told in nursery song,
To their sad history does not belong !

O lonely wanderers in the great world's wood,
Finding the evil where you seek the good,
Often deceived and seldom understood—

Lay to your hearts the plaintive tale of old,
When skies grow threatening or when love grows cold,
Or something dear is hid beneath the mould !

For fates are hard, and hearts are very weak,
And roses we have kissed soon leave the cheek,
And what we are, we scarcely dare to speak.

Father of all the nations formed of men,
Thy will be done !   Hold us beneath Thy ken,
And bring the wanderers to thyself again !

Pity us all, and give us strength to pray,
And lead us gently down our destined way !
And this is all the children's lips can say.

HAUNTED CHAMBERS.

No need have we of wizards' art—
  Of fearful charms and spells enchanted—
While loves and fears the human heart,—
  To show us chambers haunted.

For soul and sense have wood and stone,
  When wed to human recollections:
We round them with a burning zone,
  Formed of our best affections.

Our haunted rooms are everywhere ;—
  Not only where some mighty sorrow
Has girt us with a black despair—
  A night without a morrow ;—

Not only where some dear delight
    Has set our hearts and pulses bounding,
Till eyes enchanted shunned the sight
    Of all—our heaven surrounding.

These are not all the chambers dear,
    The nameless, unforgotten places
Where linger by us, month and year,
    The haunting forms and faces.

Along the highways of all lands—
    Among the streets of crowded cities,—
In hostels free to all commands,
    Save penury's and pity's ;—

In common rooms, where all have right
    To tread, with little heed or warning,
And where the guests of overnight
    Are gone at early morning ;—

By tables, where we sit at meat—
    Sit, with our food almost untasted,—
Because we find a vacant seat
    From which some friend has hasted ;—

F

In parlours where at eve we sit,
  Among the music and the dancing,
And miss some lip of genial wit—
  Some bright eye kindly glancing.

Oh, meetings on the world's highway
  Are very dear and very pleasant :
Why cannot we, for one poor day,
  Bind down the happy present ?

These are the haunted chambers left,
  That almost choke us as we ponder,
And leave us quite as much bereft
  As dearer ties and fonder.

Yet why, in chambers where we part,
  Grow sad and sorrowful and lonely ?—
The haunted chambers of the heart—
  These—these are hopeless only !

GOLDEN DAYS OF NOVEMBER.

THE autumn chill creeps over our years ;
   The autumn frosts on our heads are falling ;
And beyond the winter of death and tears
   We can hear, sometimes, the snow-birds calling.
White hairs upon the wrinkled brow
   A truce to time will soon be waving,
While the scanty fruit on branch and bough
   But little fulfils our youth's large craving.
Thank God for a late autumnal smile
   That kindles to flame the dying ember!
Sit down, old heart, and be placid awhile,
   In these golden days of November.

Who says the best of our lives are past?
   Who says that no more the angels love us,—
While the heart of nature seems so vast,
   And her kiss of peace is bending above us?

There's a soft, warm mist on field and hill,
    Where the Indian of this Second Summer
His spirit game is chasing still,
    As he did ere the reign of the white new-comer.
Away from the happy hunting-grounds
    Whose tribes his dusky legions member—
He comes, they say, when the echo sounds,
    In these golden days of November.

Once more throw open the window-pane,
    Ere to winter's blast we bar and close it;
Unfasten the heart for an hour again,
    While this golden glory overflows it.
Sit down in memory by the streams
    That dabbled our feet in the days so early—
When the budding germs of loves and schemes
    Crept under the locks so brown and curly.
Crawl out in the sunshine, crippled age,
    Though a brighter sun you may well remember:
Oh, happy for you if your closing page
    Be these golden days of November.

Is it Summer? No! the branches are bare,
    And we listen in vain for the song birds' singing;
A calm—but a treacherous calm is the air,
    And forth will the winds like hounds be springing.

Creep in, old age, to your hearth again!
    Shut down the sash, and bar the shutter!
One autumn comes, but two will remain,
    If we trust what childhood's heart may utter!
Let the night come down with its chilly haze,—
    Let the storm beat out the failing ember:
We have looked our last on the treacherous days—
    The golden days of November.

PLEADING TO THE MOUNTAINS.

THE clouds move southward on the breeze of morning;
    The peaks outpeep their curtains, one by one;
And here one spot of golden haze gives warning
    Where soon shall flash the clear, unclouded sun.
The deep ravines, where, like a white flock folded,
    All night the fleecy cloud-wreaths sleeping lay,—
The bald, scarred cliffs, in mocking snow-drifts
        moulded,—
    All—all are veilless from the eye of day.

Here rise the mountains in their awful splendor,—
    The dream of childhood, and the hope of youth,—
Before whose very thought the heart grew tender
    When seeking for the types of trust and truth:
Here rise they—peak on peak still skyward springing;—
    The clouds their playmates, and the stars so near
That when the spheres for new-born time were singing
    The chords of earth and heaven have blended here.

Gray mountains—round whose path the tempest rages
    A thousand years, but leaves nor mark, nor scar!—
Dread sentinels along the path of ages,
    Scanning the weak world's conflicts from afar!—
Types of the Infinite—the Everlasting—
    Above the reach of human hurts and harms!—
The poor, weak wanderers by your bases hasting,
    To you in suppliance stretch their pleading arms.

Look from your awful summits, ye untrodden
    Save by the foot of reverence and awe—
Look on a world in baseness sunk and sodden,—
    A traitorous world at once to love and law.—
Sleek hypocrites, who rob with silken fingers,—
    Coarse ruffians, who assault with deadly will,—
Liars, around whose lips thick poison lingers,—
    Tempters, whose dearest favours curse and kill.—

A world, oh mountains, with its portion sadder
    That these are not alone the hearts it holds :
The dove clings close beside the deadly adder,
    And white lambs nestle in the wolf-watched folds.
Oh, better that the world were wholly perished,
    All unredeemed and hideous and unclean,—
Than battling thus the hated and the cherished,
    And graves or prisons where loved homes have been.

Look down upon us, through that purest ether
    That on your pinnacles the good inhale—
That subtle substance rapturing the breather,
    In which nor foot can tire nor heart can fail.
The mists yet shroud us here—the weak eyes falter,
    Seeking to pierce the smile behind your frown:
No light have eyes upturning at the altar,
    Save that the Godhead beams in looking down.

Give us your nature, oh ye strong and fearful—
    A nature that can suffer and endure!
Scourged by the northern winds, ye ne'er grow tearful;
    Naked and desolate, ye ne'er grow poor.
The nights of centuries, with their spectres horrid,
    Have wrapped around each damp and suffering brow;
Yet every morn ye lift the reverent forehead
    To Him before whose might the ages bow.

We falter, here, with every shame and terror;
    We have not strength to keep the onward way;
We are the victims of distrust and error,
    Or of those trusts our hapless souls betray:
We lose the pole-star while the cloud is passing,
    And follow on some meteor evermore:
We die—some heap of idle dross amassing
    Above the mine where sleeps the golden ore.

There must be, on your peaks so heavenward lifted,
  Some spot, beyond the reach of shame and sin,—
Where walk, in utter peace, the great and gifted,
  And heaven's beatitudes on earth begin,
Amid your pinnacles, all time abiding,
  There must be holds, more secret than the tomb,
Where weary manhood, from its hunters hiding,
  May rest in safety till the day of doom.

Take us, oh mountains, in your arms eternal!
  From all we fear, oh cradle us away!
Or give us glimpses of that future vernal
  Whose better hope may gild the dark to-day!
Lead us, oh mountains—if no more your blessing,—
  To follow up your peaks with reverent eyes,
Till, throned above the clouds your summits pressing,
  We see the City of the Just arise.

A CHRISTMAS HYMN.

To a Livelier Air than usual.

Enough, oh world, of sobs and tears—
    Of sad complaint, and fume, and folly,
When Christmas, through returning years,
    Brings back the mistletoe and holly.
O'er long we've hung our walls with green,
    While in our hearts we wreathed the sable:
'Tis time, I think, to shift the scene,
    Ere " Merry Christmas " grows a fable.

What though we sit at Christmas tide,
    And try in vain to call the faces
That made, of old, our links of pride,
    And filled, of old, some vacant places?
What though—I say—some forms are missed?
    Thank Heaven that yet it brings us others!
Though lips are cold we once have kissed—
    The daughters live—we spare their mothers.

A Christmas Hymn.

Sweet little Meg, with golden hair
    That o'er her girlish forehead clustered,—
May be her forty, fat and fair,
    With olive branches round her mustered.
What then?   She's nearer mate, I trow,
    For us—old boys—if hale and hearty!
At twenty years we loved her so?
    Then love her twice as well at forty!

Those years—those years—they come no more!
    No spring shall break their icy fetter!
Well, let them rest!—Time brings us more;
    Who knows but he may bring us better?
The far-off hills seem blest and blue;
    The hills we tread seem rugged ever:
Yet past or future nought can do—
    To-day's the Archimedean lever!

The past—the past can ne'er return!
    We'll bow to fate and take the present:
We'll think our coals as brightly burn
    As once the Yule log crackled pleasant.
Speed on, old Time!—we know your doom
    More swift—more sure each year approaches:
But never heed! away with gloom!
    Steam be it, since we've lost the coaches!

We've not outlived—no! Heaven forfend!—
    For all we err, the Christmas sorrow,
Nor lost the memory of that Friend
    From whom an hour of life we borrow:
But down with dismal look and phrase—
    The maudlin fancies, vain and hollow,
With sinful passions yet ablaze,
    The past all wrong—and worse to follow!

All kindly thoughts—repentant deeds—
    Live *they*—in every bosom burning,
Till Time fulfils its latest needs,
    And Christmas knows no more returning.
And then—enough of sobs and tears—
    Of sad complaints, and melancholy,—
When Christmas, with revolving years,
    Brings back the mistletoe and holly!

LITTLE BARE FEET.

LITTLE bare feet—so chilly and blue,—
　On the cold, wet side-walk patting and splashing ;
As if no north-wind whistled for you,
　And you felt not the rain drops pouring and
　　dashing :—
Little bare feet—ye may not ache,
　But our hearts grow cold with a painful shiver,
And we wish we could fold, for humanity's sake,
　Such baby feet from the cold forever.

Little bare feet—but a tiny shoe
　Your tender flesh would span and cover :—
One drop of wealth the mercy would do,
　From the cup of luxury flowing over.
But a little would wrap you in snowy fleece,
　Such as swathes the limbs of our darlings rosy,
When, bathed in our heaven of rest and peace,
　They nestle to slumber loving and cosy.

Does a cheerful fire your coming await
   In the home to which you are wearily tripping?
Are there eyes to watch, when you linger late?
   Are there hands to wipe the limbs so dripping?
Or creep you away to your nest of rags,
   In the cold, damp dens where poverty lingers—
Where life the long chain of hunger drags,
   And disease clutches hearts with iron fingers.

Little bare feet!—little tender feet!—
   The answer is here, too ready and certain;
And no hand of the wizard we need to meet,
   To draw from your doom the sorrowful curtain.
All pinched and cold from the day of your birth—
   All pinched and cold to your coffin ye travel:
'Tis a pitiful lot that, when laid in earth,
   The Power that made shall sift and unravel!

Nothing we bring from the land unknown,
   When we spring, in birth, to new existence;
And we take our failing bodies alone
   When we fade again in death's cold distance:
Oh, little bare feet! the primal curse
   Ye feel in a doom most unforgiving:—
Ye have nothing in birth—in death:—ah, worse!—
   Ye have nothing—*nothing*, through all your living!

THE LAST MID-NIGHT OF SUMMER.

I START at the door with sudden shock,
And shiver, before I turn the lock,
As I hear, far off, the mid-night clock.

The last mid-night of summer sounds,
Like a ghostly watchman crying his rounds
Or the baying of Actæon's phantom hounds.

The crickets are singing their sad refrain,
Their dirge for the summer's perished reign,
In the long grass under the window-pane.

The stars are bright in the deep-blue sky—
Bright, and many, and oh! so high!
And each looks at me with a sleepless eye.

Summers ago they looked at me
Thus sadly and long, and silently,
As if there was something hidden to see.

Summers ago, in half-affright,
I shrank away from their piercing sight,
Even as I am shrinking to-night.

Summers ago they bade me do
Something I missed, if I ever knew;
And they speak the same to-night, in the blue.

Summer is gone—the white stars say—
We kissed its dying lips to-day,
And scarcely knew it was passing away.

Summer is gone: its waves no more
Will tremble low music along the shore;
They must meet the winter with sullen roar.

Summer is gone—its whispering leaves,
Its golden wealth of garnered sheaves;
And something within us pines and grieves.

Good-bye to the hours in woodland haunts—
To the sea-side and the lake romance:
Kate will flirt no more, nor Isabel dance.

Go in, as growing years require;
Put out the ashes of young desire,
And think of sitting down by the fire.

With youth, and love, and faith, and hope,
With all that widened the mental scope,
And made us able with fortune to cope;

With Mary's smile and Madge's kiss,
And hours full maddened with lawless bliss—
The heart's true summer—good-by to this.

Look down, white stars! There is nothing to see
But the world may sound with plummet free;
And cricket, chirp on, but not for me.

Can you bring me back the summer fair,
And give me something of wrong to repair?
No? Then let the dead lie still as they were.

If Margaret's lips can kiss again,
By the alchemy of regretful pain,
Then sorrow and thought may be not in vain.

But if nothing past can ever return,
Nor lamps gone out rekindle and burn,
There is nothing to hope and little to learn.

Not deader when I lie in the mould
Shall be my sight and hearing cold,
Than in the sleep that to-night shall enfold.

Good-bye to summer!   Let it go!
Other summers may dawn ere our heads lie low ;
And if not, there have been enough, I know.

So enter the house and lock the door.
Let the stars shine on, and the cricket pour
His sad refrain : it is summer no more.

THE LADY OF THE CHOIR.

She sat within the shadows soft
That gloomed above the organ loft,
And helped to lead the choral song
That swept our souls to Heaven along.

She sang—and well I mind the words
Low blending with the organ chords,
Then swelling—sweeping far and high
Until they burst from dome to sky.

" Dear Saviour, if these lambs should stray
From Thy secure and perfect way,
Oh, bring them back from sin and pride—
Thou Ever-living Crucified ! "

I heard her sing, in days agone ;
And still that sweet strain, ringing on,
Far down the dim and darkening years,
Brought holy thoughts and sorrowing tears.

And then the words no more I heard,
That all the good within me stirred :
Another voice the anthem led :
The lady of the choir was dead !

Oh Thou whose praise her erring tongue
So many a year had breathed and sung—
Grant that the voice so silent here
In Heaven be rising pure and clear !

Those waves of sound our lives that bore
So sweetly toward the thither shore—
Oh, let them not have ceased to roll
Till home they bore her pleading soul !

If half the lambs within Thy fold
Have strayed from out the paths of old,
And some yet tread the pastures fair,—
Let *her*, oh Christ, let *her* be there !

WORDS FROM HUNGRY LIPS.

"Humph! you think you have felt and known
   Something of poverty—something of pain!
Do you know what it is when the heart is a stone,
   And the madness of hunger has seized on the brain?—
When you gaze in the baker's window long,
   *And stare at the meat-shops, ghastly and grim,
And feel like a wier-wolf, famine-strong,
   Tearing some traveller limb from limb?

"Meat!—What a succulent, juicy taste
   It used to have! That was months ago.
If I only could have some kitchen's waste,
   How greasy and sleek my face would grow!
I had yesterday a crust of bread;
   A cold potato the day before:
They say that this want and sorrow must spread:
   When shall I get a mouthful more?

" I met a servant hurrying home,
　　But yesterday, with a dainty pie :
Does she know, I wonder, how near we come
　　To murder, sometimes, and the reason why ?
Then out of a basement the fragrance came
　　From roasting fowls and from broiling meat ;
And it went like poison through my frame,
　　Till I gnashed and cursed in the public street.

" You have never felt the hunger pang ?—
　　Or only its warnings far and faint ?
Then think of the sting of the adder's fang,
　　And the torture-rack of the martyr saint ;—
Of a fiery worm that moves within,
　　Burning and gnawing the life away ;—
Of the doom of hell for human sin :
　　And thank God for the mercy while you may !

" It is worst in the morning, when you rise
　　From the door-stone or the lumber-pile :
By noon, in faintness the hunger dies,
　　And the worms are still for a little while.
Then it comes again—and sharper, and worse—
　　As the dusk night falls and the lamps are lit,
And heedless of blow, or kick, or curse,
　　In forbidden places you stagger and sit.

" I have told enough.   May you never know
    Whether my words are false or true!
Put up your purse, that is thin and low!—
    I would starve outright ere I'd beg from *you!*
Forget my story, and never mind
    What a hungry man may do or say!
Who knows but I may happen to find
    A piece of bread *this very day!*"

FOURTEEN AT THE STATE PRISON.

" THERE's iron, Tom, on hand and heel;
   There's harder iron in my heart:
'Tis long since I have dared to feel—
   Kept here from all the world apart;—
A night of guilt within my brain,—
   A black despair upon my soul,
That only changes forms of pain
   As years and decades roll.

" But yesterday—ay, yesterday—
   Had I not feared a blacker doom—
The scaffold with its grim array,
   The horrid, dark dissecting room—
But for the fear of these, I say,
   I would have dashed my fettering gyves
On every head within my way;
   So loathed I human lives!

"To-day—it may be but an hour—
    Who knows how soon the devils black,
That o'er us sway infernal power,
    A moment gone, come crowding back ?
To-day the veriest little child—
    His child who did me foulest wrong—
If it but looked on me and smiled,
    Could beckon me along !

"To-day—oh Tom, I've wept hot tears !
    They shame me, but they soften me,
And loves come glimmering through the years
    That roll above me like a sea ;—
To-day I heard a carriage step
    Clank down, and peering through the grate
Came wondering eye and pitying lip—
    Those things we deepest hate.

" I scowled upon them through the bars,
    I would have cursed them, had I dared :
They had fair freedom's sun and stars,
    While I ten feet of dungeon shared.
What right had they my guilt to mock ?
    What right had they to pity me ?
Leave Prometheus on his rock,
    Unwept—or set him free !

" But one—she passed my dungeon door,
　　The last, and dared not lift her eyes,
But kept them downcast on the floor,
　　And trembled with her weight of sighs:
She would not give the prisoner pain,
　　By looking where she dared not tread ;
But I could see the pitying rain
　　Her heaven of mercy shed.

" Oh Tom !—the wealth of raven curls,
　　Thick glossed by healthful sun and air ;
The inch-long lashes, dropping pearls
　　Her sea of pity gave despair ;
Her cheek of varying white and red—
　　First red with shame, then white with fear ;
Her brow, where love and pride were wed,
　　High-born, and pure, and clear.

" Some fourteen summers must have left
　　Their holiest sunshine in her smile,
But not a childish grace was reft,
　　Nor planted one deceit the while.
And such a warmth of pitying love,
　　Shone from her sweet eyes round the room—
I almost thought the sun above
　　Was shining through the gloom.

" They passed—*she* passed—I saw but her—
 Passed on, and let my night return ;
How long will heaven its call defer,
 Ere seraph-crowned that brow shall burn ?
Heaven ?—what have *I* to do with heaven ?—
 Are soul and body under ban ?
Who knows ?—a fiend but yester-even,
 To-day I'm yet a *man !* "

MY DIRGE IN MUSIC.

FEED my sick soul with music!—do not cease,
    Though brain grows weary and though fingers tire;
Those waves of sound are very seas of peace
    Beating on beaches hot with mad desire.
The restless fiend within my nature bows
    His stubborn head, and tortures me no more:
And through the mists of care look seraph brows
    Wearing the smile my lost ones wore.

I do not hear the chant of love and grief
    Some burthened heart wailed centuries ago
To winds that quickly strewed the fallen leaf
    O'er graves where sunny heads were lying low:
I hear my own love-angel, folding down
    Her snowy wings beside a moss-grown tomb,
And singing o'er me, when the flowers are brown,
    Some lay she sung me in their bloom.

Her kindly hand has slipped its loving hold:
I reach toward her, but I reach in vain:
My hair is graying, and my heart grows old;
There's doubt and darkness gathering in my brain.
The thought of what I am stands ever near—
A mocking shade of what I was to be;
My angel only whispers when I hear
Some song of wailing over me.

There's not a plaint but pierces to my heart;
There's not a sob but stabs some darling pride;
Long wasted years from dull oblivion start,
And honours live that in dishonour died.
The good upbraid me in those pleading tones;
The evil sue for pardon and for rest:
A God again my atheist heart enthrones,
And good in suffering stands confessed.

O'er many graves the mossy marbles shine;
O'er many perished lives the sad winds wail;
But who has known a sadness like to mine—
Counting the pulses as they faint and fail,—
All time an ocean, where I float away
Beating with powerless hand the angry surge;
And music's fingers seeming but to play
One long, sad, lonely wail—my dirge.

THE PRINCE OF WALES AT WASHINGTON'S TOMB.

In the golden sun of the early October,
    By the wild Potomac's yellow flood,
At the tomb of the great world's noblest sleeper
    A group of strangers silent stood.

Full many a foot the path had trodden—
    And ever with slow and careful tread—
The path sweeping down from the house to the river,
    That passes the tomb of the mighty dead.

Full many an eye through the iron grating
    Had looked on the marble coffer gray
Where a nation, half a century younger,
    Laid the gem of their pride in dust away.

All nations, and colours, and habits, and races,
   Had made it a spot of pilgrim tryst,
Paying homage to valour, and wisdom, and goodness,—
   No blood and no climate can ever resist.

But here was a group from the Isle of the Ocean—
   The rocky isle of our fathers' birth—
The isle whose drum-beat circles and startles
   The echoes of morning over the earth.

And one was a boy, with the hair of the Saxon,
   The bright blue eyes of the German land,
Who will hold, some day, if the fates are propitious,
   The sceptre of George the Third in his hand.

Behind him were men of the proudest title—
   The feudal princes of English boast,
Standing ever around that stripling royal
   As the great ships guard their native coast.

Victoria's son—hight Albert Edward—
   He had stood already, in years so few,
On many a spot made famous in story—
   On Naseby, and Barnet, and Waterloo;—

The spots where a dynasty tottered and crumbled,
    Or a rebel baron in ruin fell,
And where, over startled and shuddering Europe,
    Rang out the great Corsican commoner's knell.

But never, I ween, on a spot so pregnant
    With varying thought, stood the boy before;
And what must have been the mingled colour
    That his young reflection silently wore!

Before him the dead lay—helpless, but mighty;
    Around him was stretching an endless chain
Of hills, and plains, and crowded cities,
    And rivers laughing on to the main.

This golden land had once been a jewel
    That flashed and glittered in Britain's crown,
His own great-grandsire had ruled and lorded
    Wherever the visitor's foot came down.

The man that was dead, in the century faded,
    Had won a wreath for his manly brow
That a hundred years ave but budded and brightened:
    Did the royal boy remember *how?*

By wresting this land from the grasp of England;
  By tearing the New World's fetters away,
And teaching the earth that long-needed lesson—
  There's no patent for heroes in royal clay.

Did the royal boy these things remember?
  And if he did, let us hope and believe
That he saw far beyond the jealousies narrow
  That national fools still foster and weave.—

That he thanked the Ruler of States and of Nations
  For the issue the dead man's valour gave—
The issue his spirit yet mournfully watches,—
  And preferred a free friend to a sullen slave.

Did he do so? Royal Albert Edward
  Alone must be called to answer for *that!*—
Or if he thought more of his last night's partner,—
  Of Teesdale's moustaches or Newcastle's hat.

Mount Vernon, 1860.

AT FORTY YEARS.

"Wait till you come to forty year!"—

[*Thackeray*—"*Love at Two Score.*"

Four decades done.   Than Christ at Calvary older,
  Counting the sea-sand years that ebb away ;—
With unseen hands that 'gin to press the shoulder
  And unseen fingers twining locks with gray.
With saucy crows'-feet that will not be chidden—
  Birds of ill-omen—tracking cheek and eye ;
Wrinkles and roughness coming much unbidden
  And proving friends by never passing by.

With much of life's great wealth most sadly wasted,
  And something better spent than brokers knew ;
With nearly all earth's pains and pleasures tasted ;
  With much proved false, and much—thank God !—
    proved *true.*
Enough beyond the crest of life's mid-mountain
  To see the eve much nearer than the morn ;
And parched in deserts, so that no cool fountain
  Shows its oasis, but some joy is born.

Learning to *live*, perhaps, the truer, better,
   Because the days of life grow few and brief;
Galled less and less by earthly bond and fetter,
   Because so soon may come the long relief.
Solving the problem of existence, only
   To leave it ere the true result appears;
Yet blessed, that fate foretells no wandering lonely,
   Friendless and tottering down the vale of years.

Deceived, discouraged, sick and disappointed,
   When early hopes come back, so unfulfilled,
The schemes best laid all scattered and disjointed, .
   The goblets of life's nectar jarred and spilled;
The "might have been" a far-off mocking vision,
   Too late to reach, now, ere the worn limbs tire;
And that most fearful mockery, self-derision,
   Sounding at every unfulfilled desire.

And yet not wretched—no! nor dully placid
   With that drugged brain that disappointment brings:
The tooth yet touches with a pang the acid,
   Yet revels in the taste of sweeter things.
With so much lost—what then?—not all is sorrow:
   Not all is lost while still so much is won!
There are, who would not change for crowns to-morrow,
   If that which has been must be all undone!

And old? Oh no, not old!   The heart of twenty
    Out-lives the changing flesh that made its bond.
Some tingles of the blood still left!—ay, plenty
    For all the tempting hours that lie beyond.
Keep the heart young, though every sinew falters!
    Keep trust in human kind, though faithless half!
And burn, sometimes, even upon age's altars,
    That incense of eternal youth—a laugh.

1863.

ALONE IN THE HOUSE.

It is midnight, solemn and lonely :
    I stand on the threshold stone
And think that without is life only,
    For within I shall be *alone !*

The door opens slow on its hinges
    And shuts with a hollow clang ;
And the spirit low shudders and cringes
    As if a death-summons rang.

In study and parlour and hall-way
    Seems the silence to gather and brood,
With the desolate feeling that alway
    Comes o'er us in solitude.

Where are they—the feet and the voices
   That echoed but yesternight?
In what far land mourns or rejoices
   The Home that has taken flight?

Are they dead?   Not so—for no mourning
   Is seen upon window or door,
And we look for their home-returning
   When the carnival summer is o'er.

But sad—oh, sad are the places
   Of our daily loves and cares,
When we think upon absent faces
   And look upon vacant chairs.

A lonely seat at the window
   And lonely the pillow white—
Because there is no one to hinder
   Or torment, or say " Good-night!"

We may chide sometimes—no matter,
   Time brings its revenge to all:
What would I not give for the patter
   Of little feet in the hall?

All silent—all sad!—No, listen!
 How the dead the living can mock !
With sad tears my eyeballs glisten,
 As I catch the tick of the clock.

It was wound by the hands that are vanished ;
 It is something they leave behind :
To-morrow that sound will be banished
 And all will be blank and blind.

And so to my rest—I only
 Of a household happy and bright :
Oh Heaven, I am so—so lonely,
 I have bidden the *clock* good night !

They will come again !—God save us
 From losing this blessed thought,
And restore the dear ones He gave us,
 With the roses absence has wrought !

A PARTING SUNSET.

THE wide world owns the sunset clear,
  And thousands gaze on its glories bright ;
But for once there is something holier, dear :
  The sunset belongs to *us* to-night.
You in your quiet summer home,
  I flying away through forest and town,—
Though far apart, together will come
  To see the last Summer sun go down.

I look through the pane of the flying car,
  And over the Highlands, low in the West,
I see the bright orb sinking afar
  Through a sky that glows like the isles of the blest.
You stand, I know it, baby mine !—
  Out by the play-house and the swing,
Watching above the tree-tops' line
  The last good-bye of the summer-king.

You are thinking of me, and my spirit ear
 So keener far than the organ of flesh,
Your " Good-bye, Papa ! " listens to hear,
 As it drops from the sweet lips rosy and fresh.
I am thinking of *you*—do you know how much?—!
 Strange child who around my heart have twined
Till mirth or tears will start at a touch
 When your elfin face comes back to mind?

How much ?   Let the sob in my choking speech—
 Let the tears that gather, and glisten, and fall,—
Tell how fondly and far the heart's tendrils reach
 When it thrones an idol and makes it *all !*
Let this childish burst of bitter grief
 At the thought : " If I never should see her more
And *her* sun should go down in an hour as brief ! "
 Sound feebly that sea without a shore !

The last clear tremble of molten gold
 Has gone : far upward the sunset ray
Tints the clouds like banners wide unrolled
 O'er the bier of the summer passed away.
Go in, dear child, to your guiltless sleep ;
 And the angels drop from some happy star,
A guardian watch o'er your pillow to keep,
 That my eyes cannot hold in their flight afar !

1863.

A WRECK ON THE STREET.

I was crossing the street, with my labour not far,
    And the care of the day hanging yet in my brain,
But with night, that was coming, set up like a star
    In the great weary heaven of travail and pain:
And she passed me so close that the fringe of her shawl—
    Her poor, faded shawl—and the skirt of her gown,—
Touched my limbs with their wretched and negligent
      fall,
    As they often had swept the worst pave of the town.

Long years had gone by since I met her before—
    Years that faded my hair and set lines on my cheek;
But the change upon *her*—oh! the fiends nevermore,
    If they wail without ceasing, have power to speak!
She was throned on the summit of beauty and pride,
    With the world under foot and the stars round her
      brow:
She was something for ribalds to loathe and deride—
    All lost and degraded and reprobate, now.

Nights of wassail, and riot, and blackening sin,
    Had burnt out the light from her diamond eye ;
Days of hunger had shrunken and shrivelled her skin,
    On whose marble the gems used so loving to lie.
Who once had not prayed for the touch of her hand,
    And thought that her breath bore the perfume of
        Ind ?
Who now would have touched her, at any command,
    Or dared the thick plague of her breath on the wind?

And this was the foot of that ladder of vice
    Of which once I had seen her on dizziest round !
With a slip of the foot on prosperity's ice,
    She had fallen so low that no plummet could sound.
What agonies—tortures,—what struggles and tears,—
    What prayers and what curses, both blended in one,—
Must have passed, through those bitter and wearisome
        years.
    While the asp at her heart its black errand had done!

I saw in that glimpse, as if lightning had shown,
    The silks that had wrapped her, slow fading to rags;—
The hands, base and baser, by which she was thrown
    To a crust in the gutter—a bed on the flags.
Saw the pawnbroker's den—the cold prison—the court
    Where justice sits striking its blows in the dark,—
Where the heartless turn sorrow and squalor to sport,
    And shame crushes out poor humanity's spark.

I saw these as I saw her : thank Heaven o'er all
    That her dim, bleary eyes had forgotten my face !
There are some we would drag to the dust when we fall:
    There are some we would spare in our deepest dis-
        grace.
So she passed on her way—that poor wreck of the past,—
    And I to the wreck that may easily be :
Who knows or can measure the level, at last,
    To be struck, in the ages, for her or for me ?

BIRDIE.

WHERE the sunshine plays above her,
　　Stolen from her sweet blue eyes,—
Where the oak trees nod and whisper,
　　Little Birdie lies.
Though the sods lie thick and heavy
　　O'er her baby lip and brow,
Yet they never—never hide her:
　　We can see her now!—

See her, as yestreen we saw her,
　　With the eyelids drooped so low,
With the tiny hands soft folded
　　On her burial snow—
See her, with the light scarce faded,
　　With the breath scarce wooed away,
That while here still kept her—*angel*,
　　And that left her—*clay*.

Why she came, a thing of beauty ;—
　　Why she fled—so brief enjoyed ;—
Why in sweetest mould created
　　Thus to be destroyed ;—
These are things that task our wonder ;
　　Things o'er which we weep and sigh :
We shall know, in after ages—
　　Know them by-and-by !

But our hearts are sore and saddened,
　　And one little mound of earth
Hides the whole world's seas and mountains—
　　Hides all love and worth.
Through the dark we grope and struggle ;
　　She is with us, everywhere ;
But the hands we stretch to clasp her
　　Only grasp the air.

Tell us not of resignation ;
　　That may come in after years,
When our hearts are water-courses
　　Channelled by our tears.
We must weep, and sigh, and murmur,
　　While *our* loss is all we feel,—
While the wound is fresh and bleeding,
　　Only time can heal.

Yet not all is loss and shadow ;
  Something from the wreck we save :
Earth's broad breast is richer—dearer—
  That it holds her grave.
And, perhaps when years have faded,
  Faltering towards the Better Land,
We may find the clue of Heaven
  Held in Birdie's hand.

LILIAN HOWARD.

I READ it, carved on a little white stone,
  In the grave-yard's shades so holy and deep,
Where nestled away lie the children alone—
  The poor little lambs of the world's lost sheep.
It was " Lilian Howard," and nothing more :
  The grave was only a yard of earth :
I had never heard of the name before ;
  I knew not her age, or her race, or birth.

But the name was full of sad, sweet thought—
  Of Arundel's line and Norfolk's blood,
Four centuries back from the Howard brought
  Who with Richard the Third on Bosworth stood :—
That blood so rich, and clear, and old,
  That in England's peerage first it stands,
And sculptors have found earth's purest mould
  In the shape of the Howards' fair white hands.

Beside that surname pure and proud
  Was the sweetest word ever mortal breathed,—
Some sweet June day, that knew not a cloud,
  In a poet's brain from the lily wreathed:
A name of purity, beauty, and joy,
  That like silver streams in music drips,—
That like the kiss of some ardent boy
  Lingers long ere it drops from the loving lips.

Sweet " Lilian Howard ! "—in that name,
  If that name was all of the charm she bore,
A shield should have stood from the archer's aim,
  For beauty and heaven link evermore.
What hearts had ached, when the sweet lids' close
  Told a love incarnate passing away—
When, like folding the lily and shutting the rose,
  Her young life went out with the dying day ?

I know not—perchance I may never know ;
  For our own griefs choke the pitying heart:
And our tears so fall in a selfish flow,
  We have none for some other's sorrowful part.
But " Lilian Howard "—sweet, spotless name,
  As it stands on that gravestone little and white,
Will often come back like a beautiful dream
  In the thoughts of day and the visions of night.

NOON AT THE BLACKSMITH-SHOP.

I SIT on the bench in the sunshine—
   On the bench by the old shop-door,
With the country's quiet around me,
   And forgotten the city's roar;—
On the bench of timber oaken,
   With its legs of many a crook,
Hewn out from the hickory saplings
   From the hillside over the brook.

The blacksmith has gone to dinner,
   With a screw-bolt left in the vice,
And the shafts of the cart unfinished
   That he promised to do in a trice.
The hammer lies on the anvil
   That no more with its battering reels;
And a daring chicken is swimming
   In the trough where he hoops his wheels.

The coal-house door is open,
　　And I see that his stock is low :
He must soon expect the coal-man
　　With his face of grimy woe,—
With his team of half-starved ponies,
　　And their harness mended with strings,
And a settlement very careful
　　Of the bushels of coal he brings.

There's a plough half over the door-sill,
　　With the coulter crooked to a hump ;—
It has been in a bad collision
　　With a stone-heap or a stump :—
A harrow in want of a dentist,
　　A wagon divided by two,
And a pile of wheels and axles
　　Grown old before they were new.

There are horse-shoes over the window,
　　And hame-sticks over the door,
And the names of the different owners
　　Chalked up like a tavern score.
O'er the beams there are bars of iron ;
　　Here's the box of tools he will use
When he fits, like an iron cobbler,
　　The horny hoofs with shoes.

There are nuts, and burrs, and ringbolts
  Lying here on the trodden ground,—
Some half covered up, till I wonder
  If the tithe will ever be found.
And some of these iron fragments
  That off from the anvil fly,
Taken up by inquisitive fingers,
  Have been suddenly dropped with a cry.

The forge is heaped with cinders,
  With a little of smouldering coal,
And I own to a strong temptation
  To pull on the bellows-pole.
I think I could manage the apron,
  And I'm not afraid of the tongs ;
I've a faint idea of welding,
  If I knew where that iron belongs.

But I've heard of people who meddle,
  With an iron too much in the fire,—
And who manage to make things warmer
  Than they either expect or desire :
I must leave the bench and the sunshine !—
  When the smith comes back, I'm afraid
He will roast me over his furnace
  For learning too much of his trade.

THE RHYME OF THE SLIGHTED
DAUGHTER.

" Never a poem for *me*—remember it father—
   While round you scatter the gems of labouring thought!
While round the heads of others cluster and gather
   The pleasant wreaths in the garden of poesy wrought!

" If you have fame, others will treasure and share it ;
   If with a name you float on the tide of years,
Proudly beside you others will brave and bear it :
   Never amid your words *my* name appears !

" My sisters' wreaths are green, beside my mother's ;
   And even my brother's, years ago in the clay :
Say, am I less to you than all the others,
   That thus my thought from your dreams is hidden
     away ? "

Ah ! is it so, my daughter ?   You—you only
   Have I neglected when the heart-dew fell ?—
When my brain was sad or my heart was lonely,
   And into words the crowding thoughts would swell ?

Were you ever pushed aside when the pool was troubled,
   With no hand outstretched to lead you tenderly in?
When words from the smitten rock in mercy bubbled
   Had you no cup the freshening draught to win?

Alas! it may be so! How vain and hollow
   Then, are the names of poesy and song,
When the words we write so little our hearts will follow,
   And our dearest loves are touched with neglect and
      wrong!

Come nearer, girl! lay close to my cheek your tresses—
   Your clustering tresses that mock the silver of age,
And see if the father's *heart* neglects or blesses,
   Whatever the words that lie on the printed page.

There are poems, girl, the sweetest and the dearest,
   That the pen ne'er moves to write, nor the page
      receives:
Such poems of prayer, oh, God!—as Thou only hearest
   When over his children's sorrow the parent grieves!—

When toys flung down from play are gathered and
      hoarded,
   And kissed at night when the room is still and
      lone;—
When the pencil-scrawls by baby fingers afforded
   Hear over them breathed love's softest, fondest
      tone!—

When the good-night kiss by the budding lips is given,
    And treasured always as one more pure delight;
When the anxious thought would measure their road to
      heaven,
    Or seek to render their earthly sunshine bright!

All these are poems, my daughter!—poems unwritten,
    But ah, how truer than all the pen records!
And how little we know, till the household circle is
      smitten,
    How deep was the music that never was set to words!

Never a poem for *you?*   Oh yes, my daughter—
    The poems of daily life and daily love,
Sung low, as the river sings with its rippling water,
    Unnoticed here, but heard in the calm above.

And see!—the things we bewail are mocking our sorrow,
    For they cure themselves as we syllable our fear.
Toil even from indolence fresh strength can borrow!
    In excusing itself your written poem is here!

EARLY SONGS.

THE Songs that burned within the breast,
  And trembled on the tongue
When life was all that bright and blest—
  That dear delusion—young!

The Whisperings of the Olden Heart
  That has no being now :
The glory of Life's better part,
  In prayer, and song, and vow.

The Thoughts recorded in old time
  For gentle eyes to read,
That looked upon the poet's rhyme,
  And never saw his meed.

The Hopes that sprung from Heaven first,
  And, dark with many a stain,
Still keep the flowers of Eden nursed,
  And turn to Heaven again.

FRANKY'S BELLS;

AS HIS SWEETHEART TOLD THE STORY.

I.

" FIVE months ago, when summer
   Lay broad upon the land,
And we were gathered far away,
   A joyous summer band,—
There came to me a little boy
   Who lisped the words of four—
Who crept within my girlish heart,
   To leave it nevermore.

II.

" Pure little soft-eyed darling!
   So pure, heaven's signet, set
Upon his baby brow at birth,
   Undimmed seemed glistening yet!
The idol of a happy home!
   The hope of coming years!
How can I speak wee Franky's name,
   And not grow blind with tears!

III.

" How in his hours of fondness
 He held his little hand
So close against my folded dress,
 And prized my least command,
Oh, child of love, and faith, and hope!—
 For fear that we should part,
So close you held my changing robe :
 How close my changeless heart !

IV.

" One day, far up the hill-side,
 I went, by wood and burn,
Till long beyond the supper-time
 Delayed my home-return.
Then, calling me, his childish voice
 Faint sounded o'er the dells ;
And lest I should be lost, he rung
 His chime of little bells.

V.

" And then he told me, proudly,
 That when he grew a man
And all his ships with wealth came home
 And strength and life began,—
I should be sister, aunt and wife—
 All loves together rolled—
And have a silver chariot,
 Its horse-hoofs shod with gold !

VI.

" Five months have passed.   White snow-drifts
   O'erlie the summer lawn.
The chariot's come, but not for me!
   Our dear old boy is gone.
One thought alone is with me now,
   By that sad memory given:
Oh, Franky, Franky!—ring your bells
   To call me home to heaven!"

Christmas, 1864.

MY SCHOOLMISTRESS.

I AM not a small boy, with his infant annoy
    But his bright, happy heart with more happiness
        swelling:
Such a claim should I dare, sure the frost in my hair
    Would a different story be painfully telling.
Nor an urchin at school, growing just beyond rule
    Yet needing it more because wilder and older,
And seeing love-wings, (those most beautiful things!)
    Sprouting forth every day from some little girl's
        shoulder.

I am neither of these: I am stiff in the knees;
    I am too old for learning, however I need it;
And a bell of less cheer than the school's I might hear
    If I was not too busy or careless to heed it.
Yet a schoolmistress fair gives me tenderest care
    And demands close attention to books and my duty:
She makes sauciest claim to my house, heart and name,
    And pays me sweet toll for her youth and her beauty.

BLOSSOM AND SUNSHINE.   *Page* 121

Bright-eyed, every day, goes my Sunshine away,
    Broad-shaded from sun or wrapped up from the
        winter,—
To the family large she has taken in charge
    To play awful Nemesis, Athena and Mentor.
With her eyes scarce so bright she comes back ere the
        night,
    Her queer little brain all set puzzled and whirling,
Till sometimes we half dread that the weight on her
        head
    Will press out from her dark locks the hyacinth
        curling.

How her warm, cheerful face lends the school-room a
        grace
    That it seems to have borrowed from sunshine and
        roses!
How the culprits look down when she thunders a frown,
    And kiss her good-night when the penitence closes!
And how bliss seems to fall, with one ready at call
    To level the sexes and laugh at the college:—
Who could tell, with small task, if I happened to ask,
    The pomologist name of the old Tree of Knowledge!

But I earnestly hope she'll not shrink to the scope
    Of dry mathematical problems and sections,
Till she goes beyond reach of the figures of speech
    And fills up all the place of the dearer affections.

And I specially pray that some possible day
   When a lover his passion may whisper and stammer,
His poor heart she'll not break for his rhetoric's sake,
   Or reject him because of a flaw in his grammar.

My schoolmistress!—bless every fold of her dress
   That so daintily sweeps round her trim little figure!
Bless her walk, every day, in that difficult way
   Which leads to true womanhood's stature and vigour!
Bless her joy and her grief!—bless her pain and relief!
   Her labour and leisure, her tears and her laughter!
What of others she learns, bring them pleasant returns!
   What she teaches, yield fruit for a happy hereafter!

1865.

FORTY-FOUR GUNS—A BIRTHDAY SALUTE.

Once I was " on the stocks,"
  (Like a plank on the carpenter's trestle),
Being shaped, from the rudest of blocks,
  To the size and the form of a vessel.
(Is there any reason therein—
  I am sometimes forced to wonder,
Why my " stocks " ever falling have been,
  And beggared my wallet of " plunder " ?)

Well, as I began to say—
  My timbers and beams wide-branching,
There came, perforce, a day
  For clearing the " shores " and launching;
And at last unveiled I lay,
  What the workshops of time deliver,
A shallop, afloat and astray,
  On the tide of the world's wide river.

I grew (as the novelists say,
    This part must be hurried briefly)
Through pain, joy, work, study, play,
    (Though the pain and the idleness, chiefly) ;
A gig, a pinnace, a yawl,
    A long-boat (six feet, very nearly),
Broad-beamed, strong and staunch, though through all,
    I was chiselled and hammered severely.

Then at last, as the years went by,
    I outlived the weary non-age ;
Manhood's spars went branching high,
    And the world confessed my tonnage.
I was twenty-one, my rate
    A sloop-of-war, thereafter ;
And master and master's-mate,
    Climbed aboard with significant laughter.

O, the many years since then !
    O, the voyages begun, not finished !
O, the stores filled and beggared again,
    And again and again replenished !
O, the days on a summer sea !
    O, the nights 'mid the waves of winter !
O, the rocks frowning close under lee,
    And the wrecks leaving shread and splinter !

And yet, I have kept afloat ;
  How, He only knows, the Great Captain,
Who the sailors in Galilee's boat
  His love and his mercy wrapt in !
And still I have grown, and grown,
  In size, as more old and battered,
Till another rate I have known,
  That I claim ere the title is shattered !

I'm a forty-four, to-day !
  That vessel, howe'er you rig it,
Lays claim to the place and way
  And the manning of *a frigate.*
So room for my towering spars,
  And the torn old sails they are spreading !
Plug leaks, paint over the scars,
  And away with doubting and dreading !

No higher rate, henceforth,
  On the books where my place was minor ;
For never to me, on earth,
  Comes the seventy-four of a liner.
Nor a sixty—and yet, who knows ?
  The old ship—God's hand is around her,
And there yet may be glorious blows
  Ere the flag goes down and I founder !

K

Only this I ask—*Stand firm*
   The crew on my deck enlisted !
And my timbers shall dare the worm,
   And the blows so long borne and resisted,—
Till the Great High-Admiral's call,
   When the fleet takes its final position,
Shall give the last order to all,
   And put me out of commission !

1867.

A SERENADE.

" COME with us, Tom !—there is beauty, to-night,
  To be stirred in its warm and rosy nest ;
There are eyes, shut soft as the evening light,
  That must wink and wonder in broken rest.
Come with us—I see that you understand :
  Half won—only half—is my brown-eyed maid ;
And I mean to behold her lily-white hand
  Waving out, to acknowledge our serenade.

" What ! shivering, Tom ?   If I did not know
  That your heart is pure as your nerves are strong,
I should think that the person trembling so
  Had suddenly thought of some bygone wrong !
What ! paler still, at the very thought
  Of midnight and music under the moon ?—"
" Hush, Ned !—take a hint, as a dear friend ought !
  I shall be calmer, you wiser, soon.

" 'Twas a night like this, Ned, soft and calm,
　　With the stars like peeping angels' eyes,
And the moonlight seeming to fill with balm
　　The whole wide heaven—earth, air and skies ;
A moonlight of only six years ago,
　　But so far away that you never heard
What changed a whole life at a single blow,
　　And made what you speak a forbidden word.

" I loved—the sweetest, tenderest thing
　　That lived, I think : very young, very fair ;
And so pure, that if words to my lips would spring
　　To tell of my passion, they perished there.
Yet some time I meant to be bolder far,
　　And to win her and wed her if heaven would be
So good as to send that one bright star
　　To make light and music and heaven for me !

" That night, the love that I dared not tell
　　In words, I would breathe in an humbler way,
With the flute's low notes and the viol's spell
　　And the harp-string making its merry play ;
Under her windows at midnight moon—
　　Six of us—five all helping *me*
To win what they guessed as so rich a boon—
　　One smile from the lips so fair to see.

" We went—we played.   There was light within:
   We saw it, and thought we had been betrayed,
And that *she* was awaiting the merry din,
   And laughing, perhaps, at our serenade.
We played—so long, but no signal came:
   No window opened, no hand would wave;
And one suggested—'twas wrong and shame!
   We might play as fitly beside a grave!

" Hark! yes, there *was* stir!   But opened the door,
   Not the window, and stood on the shadowed sill
The gray old father, whose features wore
   A soft quiet of age that seemed youthful still,
He stood there and spoke.   Ah, already you fear
   What the trembling lips of the old man said:
' Gentlemen—surely you would not be here
   If you knew—that—this hour my daughter is dead.'

" Do you wonder that years lack power to change
   That mem'ry of horror?—that even to-night
The thought makes my eyes seem wild and strange,
   And blanches my cheek to a sudden white?
Would you bid me join your number now,
   With the grief-fiends tugging within my breast—
With the charnel paleness on cheek and brow—
   A dead corpse at the banquet: a Scythian Guest?"

THANKSGIVING A-LA-MODE.

ANOTHER twelvemonths' life is gone—
Bring in the twelve-pound turkey, John!
All thanks we owe to generous heaven
For mercies held and blessings given.
Be thankful hearts in all our borders—
It is the Governor's special orders.
Who, when he hears the generous call
Laid by the guiding hand on all,—
To pause upon life's onward way,
And blessings back to Heaven repay,—
Who will desert that honoured post?
Meg, put that turkey down to roast.
Content with life, and food, and fare,
No matter what the lot we share,
And realizing, as we should,
All things are given for human good,
And all—so much from good we swerve—

Oh, better far than we deserve!
I do hope, Ruth, more nice than wise,
You haven't skimped those pumpkin pies!
*The last were—*Well, as 1 would say,
Let peace and quiet reign to-day!
Let us forget all others wrongs,
Restoring what to each belongs ;—
Dry up old quarrels, and restore
Peace and good feeling evermore.
How many are to dine, you say?
I do wish Jones had stayed away!
You know I cannot bear his sight!
Our country's day is blest and bright,
And every season wider spreads
The flag of promise o'er our heads,
And every season dearer waves
That ensign o'er our fathers' graves!
What day shall see their children slaves?
Meg, if you let that turkey burn,
I'll skin and roast you to a turn!
Who could—with plenty at their hands—
Forget dear pity's sweet commands,
Who grudge a morsel to the poor?—
Jim, drive that organ from the door!
Now rises from the fragrant dish
A savour, bearing every wish
Above this dull and darksome vale
Where grateful thoughts grow faint and fail.—

So let our aspirations rise—
But—can I—dare I trust my eyes ?—
That wing's a cinder !—to the skies.
Blest day, when round the social board
Old ties re-drawn, old friends restored—
We shut away the world's rough cares,
And trench on heaven unawares.
The turkey's ready ? warm the pie !
Now friends, with reverent hearts *sit by !*
May years that long above us roll
See no ungrateful, thankless soul !
May heaven preserve our freemen's rights,
Our morals, and our—*appetites !*

THE FIDDLER AT THE GATE.

There's a gate of iron flung open wide,
  That a certain thoroughfare overlooks,—
Through which the lawyers at high-noon-tide,
  Stream out to lunch at the pastry-cooks'.
And ever beside that gate there rings
  A musical jingle or plaintive wail,
As the old cracked fiddle tinkles or sings
  And the fiddler's fingers flourish or fail.

Poor old fellow! His coat is shabby and gray;
  And the hat that covers his thin gray locks
Has been made, in the shape it bears to-day,
  By a famous artisan known as Knocks.
And around his feet we should see, no doubt,
  Evanishing leather and draggling rag,
But that happy invention has wrapped them about,
  High up to the knees with a canvas bag.

Poor old fellow! The phrase has been used before,
  And yet repetition were little wrong;
For in view of his squalor the heart grows sore
  And the pitying eye glances often and long.
Is there anything sadder, in all the earth,
  In desert or dungeon, on sea or on land,
Than the fiddler, creating music and mirth,
  With the ache in his heart and the ache in his hand?

Whence comes he? I know not. Almost as soon
  I would ask of the Peri, fluttering down,
Where she lost from her forehead that priceless boon—
  The matchless pearl of her virgin crown,—
As harrow the old man's scaring heart
  With a question what downfall brought him here,
How far from his land he is living apart,
  Or where are *they* whom he once held dear.

From the far Green Island?—It well may be,
  For the Celtic reels ring merry and lithe;
From the Caledonian mountains free?
  Perhaps—for the strathspey echoes as blythe,
And yet, what matter? Enough to know—
  Poor old fellow! (see how the sad phrase returns!)
That his ear keeps the memory of Erin's woe,
  And he warms with the lilts from the Land of Burns!

'Gainst the rain—I own it—no armour of proof
    Guards the last of the minstrels; and yet, perhaps,
'Tis the fiddle, not he, is in need of a roof;
    And the catgut, instead of the heart-string, snaps.
Enough that when Pluvius puddles and pours
    King Richard might pine in that grim old hall,
Appealing for help to the world out-of-doors,
    And never a Blondel respond to his call.

But when the wind blows from the sharp north-west,
    When the ears grow red and the fingers ache,
When coats are all buttoned close to the breast
    And we shudder (not *give*) for Charity's sake;—
Ah, then the old man is firm at his post;
    The harder it blows, the fiercer his play:
Stiff and frozen, some morn, I shall see his ghost,
    With the glass below zero, fiddling away.

FANNY'S FIRST GRAY HAIR.

Fanny was thirty, or thereabout;
    Perhaps she might half-decline
To own, without a most beautiful pout,
    To a day over twenty-nine.
Fanny was handsome—so, at least,
    Declared that favoured glass
Which drank, in silence, that dainty feast,
    Seeing her shadow pass.
Fanny was handsome—so they said,
    Despairing lovers, a score,
Who kissed at the curls of her gipsy head,
    But wished nearer kisses, and more.

Brown-eyed Fanny came to me,
    One day, with fingers two
Holding some object so carefully
    That its value at once I knew—

Some precious pearl, some diamond rare,
   On her forehead destined to blaze :
Alas !—it was only a single hair,
   Held up to my wondering gaze !
A single hair ; but its hue, how far
   From her dark curls' glossy shine !
For its white might have gleamed, like another star,
   In the fading dusk of mine.

"See here !" cried Fanny, "a burning shame
   That work, and worry, and toil,
And striving for wealth, and fashion, and fame,
   And burning the midnight oil—
Have made me gray while only a 'miss ; '
   Good looks all taking wing !
Just look at this !—don't you see it ?—this !—
   The untimely, hateful thing !
What shall I do, in a year or two,
   When more of my youth has fled,
And half my hair has the milk-white hue
   Of this, just dropped from my head ! "

"Fanny !" I said—for a quick-shut door,
   And a step, had met my ear—
"Do you really wish to have no more,
   Just yet, of the white hairs, dear ? "

"Of course I do!" and the words were quick
  And a little spiteful, I thought.
"Then I'll tell you, girl, an easy trick
  By which the change may be wrought.
If you really wish to look very young,
  I think you will find it best
Not to lay your head too often or long
  On a gray-haired lover's breast!"

Fanny was angry: she flared like fire!
  "What, sirrah!—you do not dare
To hint that this bit of silvery wire
  Is any one else's hair!
I'll never speak to you again!"
  But she flushed such a rosy red!—
And I think that she searched and searched in vain
  For more snow on the gipsy head.
But before a month had gone, somehow
  The first white hair had grown
To some thousands, crowning a manly brow;
  And she called the head "her own."

MYSELF THAT WAS.

Gone back into the rolling ages,
  As fades some form in thickening mist;
Grown dim by slow, unnoticed stages,
  Till now no more its lines exist,—
I mind it as a thing once cherished,
  Thought worthy pride and e'en applause,
But mourned full little as it perished:
  Myself that was.

It grew in fields of boyish struggle,
  More often chilled than fed and warmed;
Its very source a doubtful juggle,
  Its shape an angel half-deformed.
A Hand, too oft unthanked, upheld it,
  In spite of broken rules and laws,
For still some Godhead memory swelled it—
  Myself that was.

'Tis easy borrowing hope from nature
　That sheds its leaves but still renews;
Though heaven has given its noblest creature
　No second spring, fresh life to choose:
Perhaps 'twas in the waking vernal
　It found that hope the sanguine draws,
And thought its lease of time eternal—
　Myself that was.

Rains on its naked head fell beating;
　Suns downward glared from brazen sky;
Cold winds dashed in with cruel greeting;
　Waves broke around it, wild and high;
The steps of succour passed unheeding,
　Nor stopped for pity's tender cause;
It fell, exhausted, broken, bleeding—
　Myself that was.

And so it faded, like a vision,
　Because it had no room on earth—
No duty, object, hope or mission
　To give existence place and worth.
And thus it sought our common mother,
　Oblivion; while, from nature's laws,
Out the crushed worm sprang forth another
　That never was.

Another—so unlike the older,
   And yet so like that none could doubt;
So wiser, sillier, warmer, colder—
   A gray-beard with a school-boy's shout;
Lover and hater—priest and scoffer;
   Traveller, with varied rush and pause:
Who knows what this shall be and suffer—
   That is and was!

Who knows what in the coming ages
   Shall be the fate of one and each?—
And what set down, on future pages,
   Wisdom by bygone loss to teach?
But Thou new life canst still awaken—
   Oh Maker! Father! great First Cause!—
In that lost hope, misused, mistaken,
   Myself that was!

1868.

OUTSIDE THE WINDOW.

Outside the window she stands—
  Outside the plate-glass with its glitter,—
Wringing her tiny brown hands
  In wishings and longings so bitter ;—
Wishing that some little toy
  From that mass of rich, costly temptation,
Could be hers—one full moment of joy
  In a life-time all want and privation.

Poor child !—to the pocket goes down
  The hand of the pitying gazer ;
For so little those wishes would crown
  And to something near Paradise raise her.
And 'tis harder to gaze upon grief—
  Harder to see than relieve it,
To hearts that God's bounty hold chief
  For the " little ones " sent to receive it.

But ah, " little one," know, as you lift
   Those eyes, with their blessing and wonder,
As if such a munificent gift
   Must be royalty's bounty, or blunder,—
Know, as the beaden-eyed doll
   On your breast finds its first childish slumber,—
We are " outside the window "—all—*all*—
   At some point of the sad years we number.

Toys that bewilder the sight
   Flash out on the wistfullest faces,
Where we children push, scramble and fight
   For the foremost, most dangerous places ;
And there in the window they lie—
   Wealth, honours, fame, fondest love-kisses,
And all that the covetous eye
   Holds dearest and sweetest of blisses.

Seldom—how seldom—he comes—
   The genie who gives what we covet :
The doll we can bear to our homes,
   Caress it, and show it, and love it.
And then—old and sorrowful tale !—
   Ere an hour the first radiance flashes,
' Two faces grow haggard and pale,
   For the gilding of one covers ashes.

Outside the window, perchance,
   May be best, if we only could know it,
For the lover, his heart in his glance,
   For the patriot—ah me, for the poet!
Only this be the boon, when all's past,
   Filling up with His mercies life's chalice:
Stand none of us, wistful, at last,
   Outside of the Beautiful Palace!

FORTY-FIVE—A GAME OF RESIGNATION.

"L'empire c'est la paix."—*Napoleon III.*

'Tis five-and twenty years ago,
   This day of March's snow and bluster,
Since I, a boy, with brow of snow
   O'erhung with locks of raven lustre,
"My Twentieth Birthday" penned—full crammed
   With words to whitened hairs belonging,—
With wails, half real but partly shammed,
   O'er cruel fate and human wronging.

I said that ere my thirtieth came,
   The grass would o'er my head be waving,
And Julia bent with grief and shame
   For that most fatal misbehaving;
I said that life had lost its bloom,
   Rubbed bare by tyrant, idiot, scoffer,—
And that an early-closing tomb
   Would be a rather welcome offer.

Ah me!—our prophecies prove false
    So oft, their very name seems folly!—
Our plans of joy the grave assaults,
    Our dreams lugubrious the jolly.
My thirty came, my thirty went,
    And I was still this side the river;
Though thinning streaks my locks besprent
    And I grew conscious of my liver.

Came "Thirty-five;" and then I called
    Old Time, the charioteer who drove me,
To check half-way, before appalled
    Some brink I reached or upset stove me;
But on he dashed, till, one March day,
    The voyager made his verbal sortie,
And trolled, in blended pain and play
    The mournful-mirthful song: "At Forty."

Four more: my fancy grew marine,
    Through summer-sailing trans-Atlantic;
And "Forty-four" might well have been
    A ward-room youngster's crazy antic.
To-day the fancy changes still;
    To Forty-five I make oblation;
And I must play, with chastened will,
    The game best known as "resignation."

The brow has lost its flakes of snow—
    They're in the hair once brown and curly;
That ugly bird they call the crow
    Has tracked my eyes a trifle early.
The young I knew are growing old;
    The old I knew have died or faltered;
The years seem short—the winters cold;
    My boot-lasts are enlarged and altered.

There's something to resign: what is't?
    My youth?—no, that is gone already.
Oh, 'tis my standing in the list
    Of able warriors staunch and steady.
Put me henceforth in the "reserves,"
    To be called out when all the younger
Have calmed their patriotic nerves
    And sated all their martial hunger.

"I do resign my office!"—So
    Old Richelieu spoke: *I* only tender
The chances I might have, to know
    The field's red glow of blood and splendour.
"The empire's peace," henceforth. Good-bye
    The draft-wheel and the conscript-ticket!
If e'er the laurel tempt my eye,
    I shall go privately and pick it.

" No cards "—if they must be *cartels*
   Inviting hostile speech and meeting.
Burst round me no more dangerous shells
   Than those that join the vinous greeting.
My sword hangs stainless on the wall :
   There let it hang, and not the owner !
And scenes of blood, when not in oil,
   Will be refused, whoe'er the donor.

" And is this all—gray school-boy !—all
   That you resign ?   Your hearing passes."
A rubber-trumpet's cheap, at call.
   "Your sight ? "   Who cares, with pebble glasses ?
" Your vigour ? "   I was always slow
   In mind, despite my body's action ;
And now the two will join, you know,
   In mutual indolent satisfaction.

" Love, hope, will, energy ? "   Not one
   That owns a year as boundary measure !
Till death the race we each may run—
   All we should *ever* run, of pleasure.
So be content, Old Time, gray elf !—
   At forty-five, with my disarming.
Yet stay !   I do resign *myself*—
   To all that lingers, dear and charming !

Ay, more—myself to chance and change,
   To stiffening limbs and slowing pulses,—
To age, with omens sad and strange,
   That effort checks and brain convulses.—
And, when there comes the final move,
   To Him who crowns with loving mercies,
And pardons, if He can't approve,
   Weak lives—including birth-day verses!

1868.

YOUR POOR OLD BOY.

With the midnight revealing his gray, bowed head,—
　With his swathed breast wearily sighing,—
With a weight at his heart like the pressure of lead
　And his throat choked as if in dying,—
Eyes scorched, not cooled, by the tears they shed,—
　Your poor old boy is lying.

Overworked, overworn, overtasked, overdone,
　Most truly and thoroughly weary ;
The past strewn with triumphs ungrasped, if won ;
　The future all pathless and dreary ;
The one voice unheard, that has power alone
　To make the dull pulses cheery.

Ah, your poor old boy is a-breaking down
    With the weight on his bended shoulders.
He feels like a motley, bedizened clown
    Turned sick 'mid the laughing beholders.
The sky is a pall, and the sun is a frown,
    And his life-hope totters and moulders.

He sometimes thinks, when the night-wind sighs,
    And these broken moods come o'er him,—
How it might have been—might have been otherwise,
    When first fate and his mother bore him;
How he might have been honoured, and rich, and wise,
    And had hope and heaven before him.

And he knows not *why* all the world's so dark,
    Just now when the light is so needed ;
When he wandered away from the saving ark,
    Or what angel to save him pleaded,
Or *what* should have been the shining mark
    Where he might have aimed, and succeeded.

He only seems to be conscious, to-night,
    That your poor old boy is breaking—
Thickened the hearing and misted the sight,
    The fingers weakened and quaking,
And nothing beyond of a morning light,
    Kept in store for a late awaking.

Ah, in such dark hours—black hours—as these,
    When both life and hope seem falling,
When the years come rolling like whelming seas
    And the chains of disease are galling,
How we learn Faust's story with painful ease
    And hear Mephistopheles calling!

Oh, to be young and in vigour again!
    Oh, to be fearful of no man!
To have grip of finger and tension of brain,
    For the grapple with fates and foemen!—
To be able to bind, with youth's conquering chain,
    The love and the faith of woman!

But "no more—no more—oh, never more"
    Will the tempter's aid be extended;
There's a boat, on a sea with a dim, dark shore,
    And in it one soul unfriended:
Row swift, row long, and ferry him o'er,
    Where the fear, with the hope, may be ended!

      *   *   *   *   *   *

Your poor old boy has been turning a leaf,
    Without waiting the light of morning—
Has pronounced Old Time but a clumsy thief,
    Only fit for detection and scorning—
Has voted Despair of his enemies chief,
    And given Mephistopheles warning.

For the thought has occurred, somewhat late, 'tis true—
    That a trifling indisposition,
An unpaid note, slightly overdue,
    And an absence outstaying condition,—
Should not fill all the air with devils of blue
    And awake such a maudlin contrition.

A cathartic; breakfast; a welcome return;
    A friend (one to *lend*, not *borrow*);
A few sheets of foolscap, whereon to burn
    Sacrificial flames to sorrow;
And your poor old boy, you'll be happy to learn,
    Will be better—much better—to-morrow.

THE FACE ON THE WALL.

BRAVE old face of my father!
  Buried now in the clay,
Yet looking down from the pictured wall,
  In the grave old, kindly way!—
Half a year has past o'er us,
  Since you quitted mortal guise,—
Since the light of the Better Land than this,
  Made bright your aged eyes.

Very lonely the places
  Have seemed to us since then—
The places where your footstep trod,
  Commanding the love of men;
And lonelier far, and sadder,
  The echoless silent hearth,
Where we seem to hear a footstep yet,
  But not a step of earth.

Brave old face of my father !
  That, when I saw it last,
The beauty of just-recovered youth
  Around the coffin cast :
Long before this, if the Blessings
  Are not fables and nothing more,
It has bathed in the light of the Great White
    Throne.
  And the waves of the Shining Shore.

And yet I sit before it,
  Dim shadow although it be,—
And dare not, cannot, will not think
  That it does not look on me—
That the eyes are dull and moveless,
  That the cheeks are hard and cold,
That the lips will never touch me again
  With the father's kiss of old !

No—let me think it living,
  Though thitherward madness stands,—
And believe that it marks my quivering lips
  And sees my wringing hands ;
And I shall not be all, all lonely,
  Though friends leave me and idols fall,—
If they only will let me think that it lives—
  The Dear Old Face on the Wall !

October 28th, 1868.

PLAY-DAYS OF YOUTH.

PLAY-DAYS of Youth, ye are gone !
  Work-days of Manhood, ye pass !
Rest-days of Age, ye come rapidly on,
  As I count the thinned sands in my glass !
Not long, as I think, ere the tale
  Shall be suddenly, silently told—
The spirit far cleaving the mist of the Veil,
  The body low down in the mould.

Play-days of Youth, did ye bring
  All the happiness due to your speed ?
Were the bird-songs all sweet, in the beautiful spring,
  All the buttercups bright in the mead ?
Or was it that then, as to-day,
  The future was charged with the joy,
And the burthen of manhood, inherited, lay
  On the tender young neck of the boy ?

Work-days of Manhood, how well
    Have the labour and toil been repaid?
Are there ingots and jewels your coffers to swell,
    And fair groves of your winning, for shade?
Or was it that, just at the end,
    The finger was weakling or dull,
Or that somebody came—foe, or stranger, or friend—
    The best fruits of your labour to cull?

Rest-days of Age, what of *you?*
    You, that of all yet remain?
Is your promise, at least, to be faithful and true,
    Or shall I be cheated again?
And yet of what consequence, now,
    Any more than in manhood or youth—
When the eyes that are flashing their light from the
      brow
    Are too dull to discover the truth?

The tinsel was bright to the child;
    The paste-diamond dazzled the man;
And the grandsire at last will be lured and beguiled
    In the very same way he began.
And what matter, again, when discerned
    Is that truth which so many has nerved—
That, throughout, more is given than honestly earned
    And less punishment felt than deserved!

M

THIRTY YEARS AFTER.

(STORY TOLD BY THE VETERAN, OVER HIS PIPE.)

It was thirty years ago,
 And I was seventeen.
Alas, what hints those figures show
 Of what present numbers mean!—
But my spirits were light, if my funds were low;
 And both head and heart were—green!

"We met—'twas in a crowd:"
 My jacket was of blue:
Its buttons would be voted "loud,"
 In this day of the modest and true;
But they were of pearl, and I was proud,
 So far as a stripling knew.

She was very handsome, and cold ;
   I was very rough, and warm :
I tried to carry her—system of old—
   In that mode y'clept the " storm ;"
And I thought, what a fortune would he enfold,
   Who should clasp her—heart and form !

Years passed.   We were husband and wife—
   How, I never was quite aware,
Except that I had an aimless life
   And fancied my destiny there,
And she lacked strength for resistive strife
   And married me in despair.

Years more.   Beside us grew
   Fair children, who linked our hands
As the young first-born, when Eden was new,
   Wore Eve and Adam's bands—
As on to the end they will ever do,
   When the love of our race commands.

And then—and then—and then—
   Who sees the dark vapour rise
That will float disease to the homes of men
   And bring Death's sad surprise ?
Nay, who sees the coming of one in ten
   Of the thunder-gusts in the skies ?

And then—and then—and then—
    Two ships on a troubled sea,
That had sailed together in sight of men,
    As consorts sworn to be,—
Drifted slowly apart, and never again
    Will look for the light alee!

And now it is thirty years!
    Ah me, my coat is black.
I have something of mirth, and enough of tears;
    And I toil, as a willing hack;
And though going ahead may have troubles and fears,
    I am glad that we never go back!

MARIE HÉLÈNE.

YES, she is dead!—you have guessed it :—
   Dead, at the moment of birth :
Only begun, and yet rested
   From all the enslavements of earth.
Formed, and cherished, and moulded,
   At such a dear, measureless cost ;
Now like a white bud refolded,—
   Love's Labour so wearily Lost !

Formed like the Medician Venus ;
   Hued of the wax and the snow ;
Dead, as she lies there between us—
   Something undreamed-of we know :
Something of birth and of being,
   Something of dying and death,
Something of sight without seeing,
   Something of life without breath.

Clay—waxen clay: is it only
　　That which an artist could shape?
If not, why thus chilling and lonely,
　　With the spirit allowed to escape?
Humanity, feebly beginning
　　To break from the chrysalis shell?
Then why, without loving or sinning,
　　Quenched by some cruellest spell?

Questions, sad questions!　Before us
　　Stretch they, unanswered and dim,
While the love of the Master is o'er us
　　And the world is not cheated of Him!
Down in the dust lowly kneeling,
　　Perhaps we may hear some reply,
When faith has grown stronger than feeling
　　And the Day-star is flushing the sky.

Yes, she is dead.　God defend us
　　From moments that harrow like this!—
In the hours of such darkness befriend us,
　　And make of such agony bliss!
Then, though the why and the wherefore
　　Puzzle the wavering sight,
We shall know that Thou livest, and therefore
　　The deed that Thou doest is *right!*

VISIBLE LOVE.

"A child is a love made visible."—*Scandinavian Proverb.*

"THREE years ago, when the flowers were in blow,
  And our hearts to each other their truth revealing,
Dear Hermann, you said that when we were wed
  You would give all the world for a visible feeling.

"The tongue might allure with words all pure,
  When the soul within had a thought unholy;
And the eyes might smile while the heart erewhile
  With sin's thick currents beat dull and slowly.

"You said you would give half the life we live
  Could the love you bore have bud and blossom,—
Could a test more rare than thin words of air
  Be applied to the truth of a lover's bosom.

" Three years are gone: we have still loved on,
  And our chain of delight has been still unbroken,
And for never an hour has the world had power
  To change or to hinder the fond words spoken.

" And often, I trow, when the sun sank low,
  And we sat at the door as the eve was falling,
The same old thought to your mind has brought
  The wish of a life for fruition calling.

" Now, Hermann, look here where our Amalie dear
  Blue-eyed—golden-curled—between us is kneeling:
Is your wish unfilled ? Has not kind Heaven willed
  That our child should be love's visible feeling ? "

BABIES BY THE SEA.

Clara and Anna and Lillian—
    Three buds of our blossoming tree,
Magical ten and nine and seven
    Playing by the sea.
Patting the beach with naked feet,
    Splashing in the brine,
Writing their names in the white-ribbed sand,
    To be washed away—like mine!

Very brave are my darlings now
    When the wave has rolled away:
They will meet the dash when the next comes in;
    They will not stir—not they!
Very weak and timid now,
    When it comes with dash and swirl
And they turn to run with a little scream
    And a toss of the flying curl.

Poor Lillian !—fate pursues us all,
　In many a doubtful shape
From seven years up to seven times ten ;
　And only the lucky escape !—
She stumbles in her sudden flight,
　The long wave seizes its prey,
And the muslins and ribbons of holiday pride
　Are limp and soiled for the day.

The tide comes higher—higher still,
　Over the beach it breaks,
And it forms in the lower sand within
　Whole rivers and chains of lakes.
Look out, small pets ! it is closing you round,
　As some darker fate may do
Before the sleep of an ended life
　Comes to eyes of brown and blue !

The causeway narrows—fly quick !—too late,
　The chance of escape is gone,
And over the sand that torrent fierce
　Of six inches rushes on.
Look up the beach—ha ! ha !—saved ! saved !
　As the theatre people scream ;
And how the curls and the ribbons fly
　As they dash through the shallower stream !

Now down on the sand, where 'tis solid and smooth,
   When the hours of revel close,
To put once more on the dainty limbs,
   Discarded shoes and hose.
For shame, old Neptune!—a wave comes up
   Where a wave swept not before,
And the children's wardrobe is all afloat,
   Going up and down the shore.

Oh, wo! what power, save fire or sun,
   Can dry those wetted shoes?
And who at home shall dare to break
   That worst and saddest of news?—
And who shall see, save the porpoise big
   As he takes his healthy sail,
Anna's garters embracing some mermaid's wrist
   Or decking some fish's tail?

Clara and Anna and Lillian—
   Buds from our blossoming tree,
The western sun is sinking low;
   Farewell to the beach and the sea.
But gather, dear ones, wherever you go,
   Pleasure as free from alloy
As that which to-day has filled my heart—
   As I looked on your childish joy!

1863.

BLOSSOM AT FIVE-AND-TWENTY.

* * * *

My daughter yet, as I like to think,
  Though seen so seldom and briefly;
Though passed beyond sweet womanhood's brink,
  And another man's darling, chiefly.
My daughter: the child of my summer days,
  Who have lain to my heart the nearest,
And found least of upbraiding and most of praise,
  Of all that were held the dearest.

How I see you, to-night, the toddling child,
  The delight of a country village,
Winning kisses wherever you romped or smiled,
  And devoting all hearts to pillage!—
Grandpapa's pet, under dear old trees
  That have long lost leaf and blossom,
While *he* hears no more the birds and the bees,
  Or the winter winds that toss 'em.

How I see you, the sweetest of budding girls,
    Half each of baby and woman,—
With long tendril wreaths of hanging curls
    That I thought something more than human!
How I see you—daughter, companion, friend,
    In the jaunts of pleasant summers,—
To places where other footsteps wend
    And that welcome different comers!

The words you used,—they come back, to-night;
    The airs you played—they ne'er leave me;
Though a shade is over their memory bright
    And e'en while they bless they grieve me.
For between us has fallen time and change:
    The dear old days are departed,
And estrangement—no! they cannot estrange
    Those who know the shibboleth—*true hearted!*

God bless you, daughter, near or far!—
    Though my hands stretch not above you
And a thousand veils may fall, to mar
    The faces of those who love you!—
Though the "King" on whose breast you lean your
      head
    Is one who "knows not Joseph,"
And though the world speak with scorn or dread
    Of lives it has known not the throes of!

God bless you!   Over the wide blue sea
   The blessing its way enforces,
So strongly that never its voyage can be
   Estopped by the west wind's courses.
God keep you!—loving heart and brain
   Ever fresh, ever bright, ever vernal,—
Till you learn of a love that knows no pain,
   In the home of the Father Eternal!

London,
   October, 1870.

III

RHYMES OF
LOVE AND FLIRTATION.

BREATH OF BALM.

CLOSE—bend close, with your soft, low whisper,
  Oh Agnes dear, in our trysting hour;
My heart hears you well, love's dearest lisper,
  And my senses bow to your subtle power.
But close—whisper close! my heart would hear you,
  As it lies in its gentle and holy calm!
But whisper close, for I drink, when near you,
  Elysian airs in your breath of balm.

Such waves of balm as my soul is drinking—
  Such gales of fragrant breath as these—
When the tropic sun at eve is sinking
  Float soft and cool o'er the Indian seas.
Such breaths come up from the strawberries dying,
  Or the ripened roses of early June,
Or rise from the swaths where the clover is lying
  When young eyes beam in the harvest moon.

N

I am old no more—nor sick—nor weary,
  As my brain reels high with this glorious wine:
The birds of my hope sing blithe and cheery,
  And the spirit of youth breathes back to mine.
I sit under trees that lost loves shaded;
  I sing old songs forbidden and still; .
I clasp dear forms that are buried and faded;
  I bound with my young life's merriest thrill.

Whisper close! whisper close! I am mad with plea-
    sure!
  That breath of balm seems opening heaven!
Filled full—running over—oh, bountiful measure,
  Sometimes to the poor and starving given!
Is it life anew love's prophet is breathing
  To the pulses so sunken, and faint, and low?
Are there chains of flowers for my senses wreathing
  Whose witchery only the angels know?

Whisper close! whisper close! the world is sinking;
  On the incense clouds of the mass I tread:
From the fount of youth I am mad with drinking,
  And the clods of my weary life I shed.
I am thistle-down;—in the air I hover;—
  I float away on a sigh and a psalm:
Oh Agnes dear you have lost a lover!—
  I have fainted—died, on that breath of balm!

DRAWING APART.

The sages have told us we number two lives,—
  The saints, that a double existence we bear;
And one from the other unceasingly rives
  That fate which we welcome, and suffer and dare.
Perhaps, merry Florence, the actions we blame—
  The actions we charge to the errors of heart,—
To mercy might lay an all-conquering claim—
  That the soul and the body were *drawing apart*.

What judge shall arraign us, with forehead of awe,
  For that which one half of our being has done?
To our poor broken fragments who fitteth the law
  That belongs to the perfect, all working as one?
Shall not Justice grow tender, and lose, at a breath,
  The scales from her eyes and the scales from her
    hands?
Poor, crippled and maimed—are we worthy of death,
  Though naked and guilty the sufferer stands?

                                        N 2

Two spirits are fighting with fury and fire ;—
  They scourge me—they rack me—they tear me in
    twain :
Two beings I bear—one hot-winged as desire,
  And the other a-weary, slow dragging a chain.
On the one, dearest Florence, spurs Duty away ;
  At the feet of the other Love lingers and pleads :
Alas ! for the promptings we yearn to obey !
  Alas ! for the fetters of duties and creeds !

Must I flee ? Shall I linger ? With lip and with eye
  Give answer, oh Florence ;—this problem work out :
But if doubts should arise, as the question goes by
  Oh, let Love have the benefit, dear, of the doubt.
And if both be our lot, let the last be the worst ;
  Leave the bitterer days to the hardening heart :
Draw nearer—love dearer—cling closer at first,
  So that death—welcome death, comes with drawing
    apart.

DOUBTING AND WANDERING.

Imitated from the Spanish.

WE sat one evening under the moon:
   The soft, cool moon, but our pulses were fire.
You said: "This is sweet, but soon, oh how soon
   Your love may sicken and pall and tire!"

Then I took your head on my heaving breast;
   I smoothed your temples, and soothed your heart;
But I could not still that vague unrest
   Which whispered you ever—"We must part!"

Time passes—the world has older grown,
   And many moons have risen and set:
But my voice has lost no loving tone—
   At the shrine once kissed I worship yet.

And you—ah well, the world is sad!—
    You ask no more if *I* shall tire:
My heart is weary—*my* brain is mad,
    Rekindling in *you* a faded fire!

Oh, Mary I, and Hazael you,
    Reversing sex, and place, and day;
For the wandering heart has been tried and true,
    And the heart that doubted has wandered away!

AN EXPERIMENT OF PARTING.

HAD I not loved you, with a burning love
  That has no type or pattern set in words,—
A love that with my being blent and wove,
  And bound my spirit with a thousand cords—
Had I not loved you, till the very air
  Bore but one blessing more than life—*your name*,—
We had not been so parted as we were,
  Nor known the joy that with returning came.

I maddened on the sweet breath of your lips;
  I fevered in the summer of your eyes;
I touched your hand, and in a soft eclipse
  My senses swooned away, as music dies.
What I had been, and what I hoped to be,
  Alike were lost in what the present bore;—
Till love and being seemed one billowy sea,
  A swimmer I, and you my only shore.

Oh, talk of bonds with which a slave is held,—
  Of fetters, tyrant-laid on free-born lands,—
Of gyves that hold, until his doom is knelled,
  With iron grip some prisoner's feet and hands ;—
They are as wisps of straw—as brittle reeds
  Beside the bonds that hold our human will,
When love's sweet calm the storm of life succeeds,
  And we a little struggle and grow still.

Alas! was I so soon a fettered slave,
  Kissing the very iron of my chain ?
Had I no life but that my temptress gave ?
  No hope but in her shadow to remain ?
Had one short absent hour already known
  A suffering difficult for life to bear ?
With what thick tortures must the future groan,
  When death, or time, or falsehood brought despair !

I saw an hundred spectres grinning stand—
  Dark spectres, bearing each a human face,
And each between us held a threatening hand,
  And mockingly forbade us love's embrace.
They pictured direful shapes on fancy's wall,
  Of which the one revealed a bridal train
And one a closing coffin and a pall ;—
  And each did coldly separate us twain.

Oh, then I knew the agony of love!
  I could not—*could not* part with what 1 *must;*
And then there grew a mad desire to prove
  That worst of pangs the future held in trust.
I could not leave you for a moment's time,
  Nor bear between us but one foot of space
So set I weary days and half a clime
  Between my exile and your heaven of grace.

Now, when the parting comes—as come it will—
  For those who closest cling must surest part—
Perchance the blow may neither craze nor kill,
  For it will fall upon a forewarned heart.
Once I have sounded all the depths of pain—
  Missing awhile your eye—your hand—your breath;
And so benumbed can wait my weary brain
  Till the last parting brings the blank of death.

THE RHYME OF EARLY LOVE.

A RHYME I sung you, darling, years ago—
    So many that since then the wearying world
Has half unstrung stout manhood's bended bow,
    And grayed the thin hair round my temples curled.
How many years, no matter ; though for each
    That date no more can fade with common years,
Than dying love forget its last fond speech,
    Or mourning love choke back the first wild tears.

Well, then a rhyme I sung you.　'Twas my heart
    Turned outward to one dear and earnest gaze ;
Concealment spurned as some unholy art ;
    The fire that warmed me, leaping into blaze.
It bore, I know it, no soft breath of Spring,
    But passion's summer-tide in every line ;
It soared, I know it, on a reckless wing,
    As if the condor's strength was mad with wine.

And then the great gift faded.   Never more
　　Have I so melted, in one draught of bliss,
The very pearl my heart of manhood wore :
　　There came no second rapture rivalling this.
Enjoyment sings its song of sweet content,
　　Or some sad omen brings its plaintive wail ;
But that wild burst, of love and madness blent,
　　Will sound no more till earth and heaven shall fail.

What then?   I think you sit with shrouded eyes,
　　Sometimes when eve is falling, breathing low
Those maddened words, and feel sad doubts arise
　　Between the present and the long ago.
" He sung me this once ! " so your heart will say :
　　" He cannot, or he will not, mate it now ! "
And then some dear hope seems to float away
　　And unseen shadows rest on cheek and brow.

And you would give, I think, a year of life,
　　If that mad rhyme of joy had never burst,
Or in the love of sweetheart, mistress, wife,
　　There once could spring some cry to match the first.
" True love is inspiration "—thus you sigh :
　　" He loved, and was inspired ; there's something lost :
He is less true, or far less dear am I ;
　　And bankrupt I must be, at either cost ! "

Dear murmurer o'er the treasures of the past
    That may be dimmed, but cannot lose their worth !—
Love's truest song is not a clarion blast
    That with its maddened joy can startle earth :
'Tis soft and broken ; faltering in its words ;
    Oft'times so low the heart must aid the ear
To catch the sweetest, dearest of its chords :
    And scarcely ever more than one can hear.

What if I sing no more at all ?   Meseems
    The poem of *our lives* is dearer far
Than any rhyme, that, bright with poet's themes,
    Embodies earth and heaven in flower and star.
Are not the trusting glance of eye to eye—
    The touch of hands that nestle where they creep—
The waiting hope when absent hours lag by,—
    Worth all the songs that shake the upper deep ?

Still read our rhyme of early love, my own !—
    Still hold it sweetly, as the bud ere fruit ;
But never let that one impassioned tone
    Drown other utterance, dearer, though so mute.
Not what we have been—what we are to-day :
    How mate to-day the birds once loving wild,—
Be these the thoughts that keep life's summer May ;
    And do not make me *jealous of my child.*

SNOW-WHITE DOVE O' MY HEART.

Oh, birdie! birdie!—from heaven winged down!
  Oh, snow-white dove o' my heart!—
Why when hither you flit must the storm-clouds frown,
  And why must we nestle apart?
I see the snares of the fowler lie low,
  And the shafts of the archer that fall:
Oh, birdie! birdie!—my heart is woe
  That I cannot shield you from all!

Shall I see your plumage of frosted snow
  All dabbled with blot and stain?
Shall I see the dear crimson life-blood flow,
  And stretch my poor hands in vain?
Shall I live for that day—that cruel day—
  When the hope, with the fear, is o'er;—
When the wings are broken and down in the clay
  And my love-mate comes no more?

Go, birdie, and sing at the gates of the morn
    A prayer that the Master will hear—
That the power may be given, from arrow and thorn
    To shelter a breast so dear !
For where will I turn, and what will I do,
    Oh, snow-white dove o' my heart !—
When the hope proves false and the fear proves true
    And for ever we shiver apart?

1864.

HOW HE LOVED ME!

SOME day when the long green grass is waving
  O'er a mound beside a burial-stone;
Or when ocean winds are madly raving,
  'Tween two parted continents making moan,—
      "How he loved me!"
  Say—thus bridging o'er the vast unknown.

" How his quick ear heard my faintest calling;
  " How his will, so stern to all beside,
" At my feet was ever lowly falling,
  " Till to *me* submission seemed his pride!
      " How he loved me!—
  " Till in *me* all other wishes died!

" How around my path, with briers entangled,
  " Ever seemed to move a careful hand,
" Heeding not how much 'twas bruised and mangled,
  " So that *I* could reach the wished-for land!
      " How he loved me!—
  " God! Thou knowest!—and *I* would understand.

" All the past, to him, seemed loss and sorrow
  " If its memories held our lives apart ;
" All the future he would lose to-morrow
  " If it did not bring us heart to heart.
      " How he loved me !
  " Hear, oh absent soul, where'er thou art ! "

Sing me this, when our brief day is over,
  By the sea, or in the churchyard's shade ;
And the spirit, round thee taught to hover,
  Sure will hear the tone, like wind-harps played.
      " How he loved me ! "
  Say—and even that love will be repaid.

Nay, suppose we change the saddening omen—
  Let the present bar the future's gloom ;
On thy lips, thou best beloved of women !—
  These words rippling through the crimson bloom :
      " How he loves me !
  " How I love *him*, answer, Day of Doom ! "

WICKED EYES. *Page* 193.

WICKED EYES.

'Tis no matter when I met her,
  Or where, or why, or how—
If the cap of queen or working-girl
  Was arched upon her brow.
Enough, that years have fled me,
  With hasty foot, since then,
And that she was worthy the respect
  Of angels and of men.

And yet those eyes were wicked—
  Oh, very Wicked Eyes,—
Within whose depths a different thought
  Each moment seemed to rise :
Now tender love and pity ;
  Now pride akin to scorn ;
And now the dawn of a subtle thought,
  Like the warming tints of morn.

o

She looked, and I was vanquished ;
　　She smiled, and I was healed ;
She frowned, and a line of daring thoughts
　　Lay helpless on the field.
She spoke, and I heard low music ;
　　She sang, and I lost my breath ;
And ever since then my life has been
　　What the good find after death !

Oh, how the dear eyes lashed me
　　With whips of stinging rays,
When I bent too low before my queen
　　Or trod in devious ways !
Oh, how they came at midnight,
　　In the quiet spell of dreams,
And chastened pride, and kindled hope .
　　And awakened poet themes !

They have made me madly jealous,
　　Lighting another's face ;
They have taken the pang from poverty,
　　The danger from disgrace.
They have blotted out the pole-star
　　That had else been singly bright,—
As flushed aurora dims the north
　　With one broad flood of light.

And can such eyes be wicked ?
  Alas, so cavillers tell ;
And a thousand friends will point me out
  That their rays are sent from—Well !—
My predestined purgatory,
  I think, will wake no sighs,
If 'tis that towards which I gladly steer,
  In the light of Wicked Eyes !

MY DARLING'S HAIR.

'Tis the Merry Christmas morning,
   With the sun shining bright on snow:
I hear the church-bells ringing
   And the horns of child-land blow.
The sights and sounds of the season
   Are jubilant everywhere ;
Each has something o'er which to be thankful,
   And I have my darling's hair !

The glossiest, darkest of tresses,
   From the throbbing temple shorn
One day when in coming absence
   New love and grief were born.
Over many a league of travel,
   To my wearied eyes and heart
It has been the dearest companion--
   Of herself and her love a part.

And to-day, as I take it softly
   From the place where it folded lies,
And touch it with thrilling finger,
   And caress it with lips and eyes,—
To-day, when the waves are narrow
   That still lengthen the parted despair—
Like the gifts of the worshipping Magi
   Seem the threads of my darling's hair.

There is light in its glossy darkness,
   As their diamonds flashed from the mine;
There is fragrance of myrrh and frankincense
   That raptures the soul like wine;
And oh, if the star is less radiant
   Than that o'er Judæa hung,
And the song less heavenly-holy
   Than that which the angels sung,—

Is it not, oh Merciful Master!
   A spark from that glory above
Which enfolds all the worshipping nations—
   Ever-born, ever-living Love!
And wilt Thou not hallow and shape it,
   And give it a name and a place,
To be part of Thy birth-day blessing
   To our struggling and sorrowful race?

What was it I heard ?   Did the church-bells
   New omen the happy time
And blend with their Christmas music
   A still purer and sweeter chime ?
Or was it the glamoured senses
   Shaping thought on the Christmas air,—
Grown wild with the subtle perfume
   That floats from my darling's hair ?

TWO AT A TIME.

I wish I could be—but I cannot, you see!—
    Still faithful to one of the bright-eyed and fair:
For they tell me a truth to which all must agree—
    That one man to one woman gives each but his share.
They say it is treason—the verdict is true!—
    Doubly worse than a fault, and approaching a crime:
But what can I do, when temptations are two?
    How *can* I help worshipping two at a time?

There is Inez, dear maid of the glossiest curls—
    Sloe-black, like her eyes, and with lips at a pout!—
The dearest, the tenderest, sweetest of girls,
    With fondness and faithfulness no one can doubt:
Not faithless to *her* would I dare to be—no!
    To the height of her love it were heaven to climb!
But *is* it then faithless if only I go
    To the modest proportion of two at a time?

For when Isabel comes, with her tresses of gold
    And eyes that are melting and heavenly blue,—
What crime would it be, if I, heartless and cold,
    Turned away from her smile, as a villain might do !
No ! I float down the stream of her kisses and sighs,
    Drink her voice like the bird-songs of tropical clime,
Nor remember, till thought brings regret and surprise,
    That my faith is divided by two at a time !

Now what can I do ? give up one ? give up which ?
    Bear the name of a traitor, to blue eyes, or black ?
Starve and shiver, when Love has a treasury rich ?
    Run away like a coward, Love beckoning back ?
All ye powers of true tenderness !—grant me the prayer
    To roll up the two in one mixture sublime !—
So that bliss with them both I may render and share,
    And the rapture of two come with one at a time !

A LEISURE HOUR.

In imitation of Sir John Suckling.

I HAVE a leisure hour! not many
   I find amid this maelstrom life.
Ah me, I know not if there's any
   Free from some duty, want or strife.
Yet here unbusied I am sitting,
   While day declines and evening falls,
And shadows changing, fading, flitting,
   Play on the dull unstoried walls.

A leisure hour. How shall I fill it
   So that some day, when looking back,
Sweet memories may, if I so will it,
   Gild that brief time's evanished track?
Warm heart!—the answer quick thou givest,
   Making my pulses bounding stir.
True heart, of every hour thou livest,
   Some part, at least, must be for *her!*

So I will think how much her presence
　　Has added beauty to the past ;
How every path has been a pleasaunce
　　If on't her foot its shadow cast ;
How softer every eve has faded
　　If her eyes saw the glow with mine,
How flowers her nimble fingers braided
　　Have almost made me drunk like wine ;

How all the sad, and dull, and lonely,
　　Have brightened 'neath her sunny smile
'Till earth has gloomed for others only
　　And Eden's light seemed hers the while ;
How e'en the hand with labour weary
　　Grew nerved again when she upheld,
And shadows fearful, black and eerie
　　Shrank back and vanished, shamed and quelled.

What witchery was't that shone about her—
　　That made me slave, yet throned me king ?
What had the sad world been without her,
　　But one huge, dismal, blighted thing ?
What hard fate held her far in distance
　　While arms outstretched and sad lips moaned ?
What blest fate gave her to existence
　　And all the weary past atoned ?

See—time has flown: my hour of leisure
   Has dwindled to at most a third,
While in my heart that sad, sweet pleasure—
   Her past—the wells of joy has stirred!
Present and future yet unspoken;
   And ere the spell of each I rede,
How can the chain of thought be broken,
   And the proud, willing captive freed?

Her present? Ah, 'twere rash betrayal,
   To other ears, of bliss conferred,
If every hour of love's repayal
   Were shaped and moulded to a word.
Her present? No—see how expression
   Can grasp a volume in a line—
Make of two hearts the one confession—
   She lives—she loves—her love is mine!

Her future. Only God in heaven,
   And the dear angels round His throne,
May know the ban or blessing given
   For days that fill the vast unknown.
Yet hope may grasp the sacred altar—
   That He, who guides the sparrow's wing,
Will let nor heart nor footstep falter,
   Till love's last sheaves the reapers bring.

So let it be, oh, Ever-Present !
　Whether the paths that yet remain
Be bright with fortune's sunshine pleasant,
　Or scourged with beating blast and rain.
Thou temperest man his bitterest weather,
　As Thou his sunshine smilest to make ;
And hearts that love can bear, together,
　What each, alone, would crush and break !

And thus my leisure hour is ended—
　Filled full of *her*—hope, love and fear ;
All things to one great key-note blended ;
　One thought, will, purpose, only clear :
To own the past of troubled blessing ;
　To hold the present, true and fond ;
And meet, with love, faith, prayer, caressing,
　The great dim future far beyond.

HUNGER THAT NEVER CEASES.

Not Ugolino, gnawing away
    At his shrivelled and shrunken and bony fingers ;
Not the starving at sea, dying day by day,
    While yet bygone food in the memory lingers,—
Not either of these have known hunger, I think,
    As some may know it, through days—weeks—ages—
Who walk the free earth, and eat and drink,
    And enjoy prosperity's wages.

For there is a bound to appetite,
    And the sharpest may soon be cloyed and sated ;
But who has yet filled with love's dear sight
    The eye that for one pet form has waited ?
And who has supplied the yearning heart
    With enough of the presence sufficing only,
So that when once more removed apart
    There should be no pining lonely ?

Oh love !—love !—love !—the hungerer's feast,
　Richer than quails and sweeter than manna,
Where the soul, participant, giver and priest,
　Dispenses, and feeds, and sings hosanna !
Oh, love, why is it that over and o'er
　As we eat we long—desire increases
With its very food—a content no more—
　A hunger that never ceases !

I ate, last evening, and was filled ;
　I ate and drank again this morning,
Till from food, Olympian-Jove distilled,
　My physical self would turn with scorning.
For I saw *her* yestere'en, for hours ;
　And I shall see her again to-morrow ;
Yet my soul is crying, with all its powers,
　Against *separation's sorrow !*

Only an hour from my waiting lips
　The banquet—and I so sick with hunger !
God !—what would it be, in death's eclipse,
　Each starving day growing longer and longer !
Or what would it be if falsehood came
　And changed her face from its light so pleasant—
With the Eden past wrapped in swords of flame
　But its memory ever present !

Oh waiting eyes! oh famished heart!
　There is one—but one—can ever fill you;
But the pang will come if you sever apart,
　And for each past joy some pain will thrill you.
Come, banquet of love, in your tempting shape!
　I fast—I am famished—the pang increases!
Give me *her*, every moment, so I may escape
　The hunger that never ceases!

AFTER THE MEETING.

Imitated from the Spanish.

I was sad to-day, that the weary hours
　So loitered on ere they brought our meeting ;
But the hopes of your coming scattered flowers,
　And a musical chime seemed the clock repeating.
I am sadder now ; you have come, and gone :
　The cup has been filled, and crowned, and tasted :
The mind has a wearier journey on
　Till again to our meeting time has hasted.

Every meeting makes it harder to part ;
　Every space between grows longer and longer ;
The chain of fire that girdles the heart
　Grows ever tighter and ever stronger.
Oh, what shall we do when the dream is o'er ?—
　When the gaze is only backward turning ?—
When the one to the other comes no more,
　And the other has lost this hopeful yearning ?

Shall we die? shall we madden? shall we smile
  In bitter scorn at a tie so fated,
And try to forget how weary the while
  Once seemed—when we trusted, loved, and waited?
Ah! Madre de Dios! grant us peace!
  Give us patient hearts for the doom of the Giver,
Whether our lives in their meetings cease,
  Or we blend in the heaven of love for ever!

HOLDING HANDS.

It was in the theatre, one night,
    Amid its blended hush and stir,—
When lamps were bright, and hearts were light,
    And I was sitting alone with *her*.
Alone—for we all have inner rings
    Within which only the dear ones come,—
Spots round which the peace-dove circles her wings
    With a privacy like home.

We were very near—so very near
    As only those can understand
Who have had fond words and kisses dear
    Blown towards them in some far-off land.
So near as only those can be
    Who have bartered half of heart and brain,
And cast off the boasted will of the free
    To hug idolatry's chain.

We saw the players, not as two,
    But one—one eyesight serving both.
We heard them speak, but the second knew
    What heard the first, of a perilled troth.
I think, over all the wide, wide earth
    No two had existence nearer blent,
Or better concentred all love's dear worth
    In one silent, supreme content.

And yet—what was it?—I seemed to know
    There was something dearer lying beyond:
More tropic warm in the blood's sweet flow,
    More loving pure, more chastely fond.
What was it?   Ah, there's a pippin's fall
    To guide the Newtons of other lore
Than that which holds the stars in thrall
    And measures the skies we adore.

A soft, warm hand fell touching mine;
    Then crept within it, finger and palm;
And a thrill in my pulse, like rioting wine,
    Was soothed to a happy, quiet calm.
I was warmed, till no blast of arctic cold
    Could chill me again, through cycles of years;
I was lapped, like a lamb, in fleecy fold;
    I forgot pains, troubles and fears.

I thought, as that touch o'ercame me quite
    And love's electric circle and chain
Drew round me, filling sense and sight,
    Enthralling heart and soothing brain,—
I thought, and the thought is with me still,
    Compelling words, as raptures then,—
How thriftless even the loving will,
    In the sons and daughters of men!

We walk together, side by side, .
    We sit together, blissfully near,
With the fond ones filling hope and pride
    And beyond all language darling and dear;
And yet the fond hands seldom close,
    Because we are watching the great world's eye,
Or because a dearer rapture grows
    In the thought of "by-and-by."

Long hours, with hands so near—so far:
    And then life's sun goes down at noon;
The night of love has no ray of a star,
    Or gravestones glimmer under the moon.
The dear hands chill in the cold, damp earth,
    Or they flee so far that reach is vain.
Oh then, heaven, *then*, what a touch were worth,
    As a break in that endless pain!

Too late!—too late!—like many things
   That we weakly essay when the chance is past!
For the hands, to me, grow angel's wings,
   Tender, and pure, and flitting fast.
Clasp close—clasp long—clasp ever!—I said,
   That night, and she answered.   Could we but know
What the grasp is worth, till the grasp is fled,—
   Would we ever, ever let go?

BLINDNESS IN ABSENCE.

Imitated from the Spanish.

Not because thy face is missing,
  With its fond and gentle smile,
With the lips that pout for kissing
  And the eyes that mine beguile;
Not because thy dear form hovers
  Near my waiting grasp no more,—
All my heart its grief discovers
  When our parting words are o'er.

'Tis because the mists are closing
  When I see thee fade away,
And thy life my soul is losing—
  Losing, wondering, night and day.
Where thou wakest—where thou sleepest—
  Through what walks thy feet may rove,—
Fast or vigil—which thou keepest—
  These are doubts that rack my love.

I could bear our sad, long parting,
   If thy *place* my soul could see;
I could check these tear-drops starting,
   If my eyes but moved with thee.
Through the halls thy feet are treading
   Let me glance, and grief will cease:
Where thy white couch they are spreading
   Let me look, and all is peace.

Give me power, oh Inez, dearest,
   But to see thee where thou art,
And the sight will bring thee nearest,
   Though in absence, to my heart.
Or if this must be denied us—
   Still this blindness shroud the eye—
Come—come back ere worse divide us!
   Come—come back before I die!

WISTFUL GLANCES.

Imitated from the Spanish.

THOSE who judge our hearts' devotion
　　Only by the words we speak,
Sound affection's troubled ocean
　　With a plummet poor and weak.
Those who by our actions measure
　　What we wish and what we feel,
Little know the pain and pleasure
　　That our lives may yet reveal.

When we meet, my Inez! dearest!—
　　Some are near, to fright the heart;—
Some I hate and some thou fearest;—
　　Ever holding us apart.
One snatched kiss may seal our meeting;
　　When the number each desires
Mocks the sands where ocean's beating
　　Or the sparks from myriad fires.

Never can the saints above us
    Who, as long years come and go,
Yet will join if yet they love us,—
    All the hidden mystery know,
Till they read those wistful glances
    That my eyes (they only free!)
Steal, in every hour that chances,
    Toward some link that binds to thee!

—Toward thyself, when heaven's best blessing,
    Presence, thou hast timely brought,
And those eyes, alone caressing,
    Do what lips and fingers ought ;—
When they follow every motion
    Given by foot, or hand, or head,
With the silent, dumb devotion
    Grey-hounds pay their master's tread.

—Toward the window of thy chamber,
    Where, so glad to peep within,
Wild vines climb and roses clamber,
    Never chidden for their sin,
I must never lift the curtain,
    When thou stand'st, in snowy white,
Half unrobed, and eyes uncertain
    In the languid drowse of night.

I must never tap the casement,
    When thou kneel'st in rapture deep,
Seeking, low in prayer's abasement,
    God's sweet peace to crown thy sleep ;
Yet my wistful glance, returning
    'Spite of prudence, 'spite of care,—
Bears a power so wild and burning
    Thou might'st *feel* it lingers there !

Spots thou treadest, gloves thou wearest,
    All once blessed by touch or sight,
Part of thee, my Inez, dearest !—
    Give my eyes this sad delight.
Come to me !   Come nigher—nigher !—
    That the wistful glance may die
Iu that feast which drowns desire—
    Lip to lip, as eye to eye !

ONE!

ONE face and form that fill the eye
    With dear delight or restless yearning;
One smile towards which, 'neath every sky,
    The gaze is ever fondly turning;
One presence—body, spirit, soul—
    That, near or absent, seen or missing,
Keeps sweet or sad but sure control—
    Makes light or darkness, ban or blessing.

One unit in the world's great sum,
    That turns to nought a million others;
One voice above the world's wide hum,
    That space may calm but never smothers;
One light upon a devious way,
    Near which a thousand flash unheeded—
Books, sermons, labour cast away,
    But one thing known, but one thing needed.

Oh, glorious, almost-fearful One,
    That so absorbs soul, life and spirit !—
'Tis no light prize that thou hast won,
    No tinsel crown thy brows inherit.
Thou wearest *me* for diadem—
    No single thing, but all belonging ;
And woe, to flaw or stain the gem
    With deed or thought thy queenship wronging !

Oh, One for whom no duplicate
    Exists in future, past or present !—
To whose white hands so proud a fate
    Is given, so fettered, tamed, quiescent !—
Know'st thou the duty thus involved—
    To wait, to strive, enjoy and suffer ;
Life-problems to be bravely solved,
    Smooth paths eschewed for highways rougher ;

Old wrongs condoned, old sorrows healed ;
    Wealth sought, in other modes than mining ;
Hot words in love's soft flame annealed ;
    The torch of trust kept clearly shining ;
And much, denied to common creeds,
    Seized with a faith that never falters ;
And much, that baser worship needs,
    Chased, scoffed and scourged from purer altars.

From marble blocks of circumstance
   Whole lives and fortunes carved and moulded ;
With nothing left to change or chance,
   But all in loving growth unfolded ;
Till through the blue, with course as true
   As once it bore o'er Jordan's river,
The dove of peace shall come anew—
   In this life, or the far Forever !

So ends the lay, oh peerless One !—
   Ends with the thought that gave beginning.
Yet pause !—the task is half undone,
   No sibyl omen sweetly winning !
No other numeral so recalls
   What lulls e'en love's keen fears to slumber :
One—*Won*—the dearest word that falls
   From human lips, when thine the number !

WHAT WILL YOU DO WHEN I AM GOING?

WHAT will you do when I am going—
    Going far away, for weary days,
With the tears of a lonely sorrow flowing
    And the world all blank to the cheated gaze?
Will you only fade and droop and sadden,
    As droops the flower when sunshine fails?
Or will you go wild, despair and madden,
    Waiting the glimpse of returning sails?

What will you do when I am going
    That road which all mortality takes,
With the mists of age o'er the keen eyes growing
    And the life-cord strained ere it jars and breaks?
Will you let me go, like a cloudy morrow
    That has darkened awhile your life's fair field?—
Or clasp me close, with a holy sorrow,
    Fighting death with love that can never yield?

What will you do when I am going—
  Going far away, to return no more?—
With the boat at hand that will soon be rowing,
  Rowing me on to the Silent Shore?
Will you quite forget the old days departed?—
  Or wait and watch, with tear and prayer,
Till you find the heaven of the faithful-hearted
  And come, unaltered, to love me there?

AN HONEST DISCLAIMER.

I DO not love you.   Never heed
   A word would give that false impression,
Or think that I shall stop to plead,
   With lisping voice and fond confession.
I would not do so, for a queen,
   E'en if I held her ne'er so dearly—
But keep my calm, unruffled mien,
   And shut my heart and lips severely.

I love *you ?*   No! forbid it, all
   That keeps the strong heart free from fetter!
And yet, lest disappointment fall,
   I'll do a wiser thing, and better.
This frank disclaimer kindly take,
   And keep its cold words still before you:
Yielding one point for pity's sake,
   I do not love you—I *adore you!*

THE LIGHTS OF LOVE.

By sunlight first I saw your smile
   Fall softening, healing, warming,
A hope of love, so crude erewhile,
   To life and beauty forming.
By moonlight first I took your hand,
   Beside a lapping river,
And wandered with you towards a land
   Of bliss to both for ever.

By starlight I have seen your eyes
   With hope and pleasure glisten,
When sweet words died in sweeter sighs
   And only hearts could listen.
And oft by lamplight, at your side,
   So full has run love's chalice
That we had more than monarch's pride
   And trode some fairy palace.

Q

And yet the dearest ray of all
    Not one of these has given;
For fonder light may beam and fall
    Than sun or stars in heaven.
Your eyes' sweet spark, seen through the dark
    In sacred hours and lonely,
Has found content a higher mark :
    Come light me—light me, only !

LOVE AT A BARGAIN.

Come with me, dear!   We have waited long
'Neath the lash of want and the grip of wrong!
We have sighed, as no raven over the door
Of a mad poet's study: "Nevermore!"—
Because 'twas more evident, as they say
To the meanest capacity, day by day,
That fate held us asunder with cruel sword,
For love was a thing that we couldn't afford.

Light your purse, love: very light mine;
And light would the weight be, should both combine.
Dreadful the pang, to be sundered apart,
With tingling in pulses and sorrow at heart;
But what would two pounds a fortnight be,
To material people like you and me,
With appetites sharpened by country air,
And the fatal requirement of something to wear?

Q 2

How should we feed and clothe ourselves?
How feed—don't hush me!—those little elves
Who might be expected, in natural course;
To add to the country's numeral force?
Eschewing ice-creams and ignoring stews,
Where could we even find hats and shoes?
Leaving out champagne with a cobwebbed cork,
What raven would bring us potatoes and pork?

You have wept, I know it—so have I—
To see the best years of our lives go by,
And think how on into white-haired age
We might beat the bars of our weary cage,
Patiently wait and sullenly mope.
Without a prospect and minus a hope,
Only sure of one thing—if Love should die,
We might buy it a coffin, by-and-by.

Come with me, dear! The riddle is read!
I lift like a monarch my drooping head!
For I've just conversed with a travelled man
Who returns from the far-off land of Japan,
And he tells me that in that radiant sphere
The palaces rent for twelve shillings a year;
That a penny a day will keep in clover
A man and his wife, and leave something over!

Servants galore at a pound a year,
A horse and a groom for a trifle mere,
And all the rest that people need
On that very moderate scale indeed.
Come, we will go—a wedded pair—
To that cheap elysium opening there,
And you shall wear tappa for robe and veil,
And I two swords and a wonderful tail.

Come! for the heart grows sick with haste
Seeing that bright hope over the waste!
Come!—to that land where nature rules
And they seem to have neither money nor fools!
Come, to the long deferred embrace,
As sprung to her lord the first of our race!
Come, to your husband-lover's side,
My fond, my beautiful one!—my bride!

P.S.—One matter there still remains,
May yet bind, for a little time, our chains.
I forgot to ask the travelled man
Whether in far-off, happy Japan,
An industrious couple, working away,
Could earn that little " penny a day,"
Or whether, house-rent and servants clear,
We might not still starve by the end of a year!

IV.

RHYMES OF TRAVEL.

THE OLD AND THE NEW.

Britain! thy boast is of the Old
   And bravely thou hast borne it!
Proud floats thy red flag, fold on fold,
   Though all heaven's winds have torn it.

In stately temples, marble-piled,
   Thou hast a thousand lying,
Who in the face of danger smiled
   And honoured thee in dying.—

A thousand more, whose tongue and pen
   The softer muses courted;
Or statesmen, nearer gods than men,
   Who thy best weal supported.

No foot can tread thy tough green sward.
　But seems, where'er 'tis moving,
To touch some hero's great reward—
　Some woman's meed for loving.

Thou art the Old—th' incarnate Old,
　Whom, scathless, few have smitten,
Since Cæsar's chariots northward rolled
　And Rome was lord in Britain.

And he who at thy shrine can stand,
　And feel no reverent wonder,
Deserves to own no fatherland
　The broad sun smiling under.

And yet there is a sweeter pride,
　Oh, Britain!—than the pleasure
Of claiming all this glory wide
　And sharing all this treasure.

The New is dearer than the Old
　Braver, and truer-hearted!
Give me the *future*, far unrolled,
　And take the *long-departed!*

Thy page is written; but on *ours*,
　Flecked by the starry banner,
A few brief words have tasked all powers,
　Dashed in the rudest manner.

Yet there is strength in every stroke;
　And when that page is ended,
Be this the verdict we invoke—
　"Right served, and man befriended!"

And if within our cloistered halls
　Few marbled heroes cluster,
Heaven!—when the trump of battle calls,
　How thick and fast they muster!

If poets' fame and sages' prayer
　Your history gild and burnish,
How can even that long list compare
　With those we *mean* to furnish?

The steed, with many races won,
　Be sure has spent his sinew;
And you, Old Britain, so much done,
　No longer have it in you!

So take the Old; give me the New,
The future and its winning;
And when you make your last adieu,
We shall be just beginning!

London,
July, 1865.

THE BLADES OF ENGLAND'S GLORY.

THEY do not hang in Windsor,
  Nor cluster in the Tower,
Red-flushed with recollections
  Of battle's shuddering hour;
They have not struck at Acre
  Or gleamed at Waterloo:
They have only looked up at the noonday sun
  And drunk the morning dew.

The blades of England's glory,
  Sprung from her generous soil—
Not nurtured with the hero's blood,
  But nursed by manly toil!—
St. George's Cross may waver
  And lose its scarlet sheen;
But there's nothing can dim the emerald flash
  Of " England's fadeless green."

A math of deep-piled velvet,
  I tread that matted sod,
And think so rich a carpet
  No emperor ever trod ;
And lonely, faint and weary,
  Could I but choose my rest—
How I'd lay my cheek on the cool, green leaves,
  As on my mother's breast !

On hill and plain and meadow
  Still spring they, fresh and strong !
The wealth that feeds her millions—
  Her worthiest theme of song !
And kiss they the feet of maidens
  That bend them as they pass :
For the blade that will conquer and rule the world
  Is the tiny blade of grass !

London,
    August, 1865.

OVER THE BRINE!

Over the brine—over the brine—
Yonder the white cliffs of Albion shine.
Faster, speed faster, to meet our desire,
Black-breasted sea-gull, with pulses of fire!
Heed not the wind that howls angrily past!
Heed not the salt spray that flies to the mast!
Faster, yet faster, good steamer of mine,
Bear us and hurry us over the brine!

Over the brine—over the brine—
Away from the land of the melon and vine ;
Away from the land where a conqueror's thread
Leaves half of a nation yet helpless and dead !—
Away from the land where God's faith seems a form,
Instead of true reverence fervent and warm—
Where traditions too close round the free heart
    entwine,—
Bear us away from it, over the brine !

Over the brine—over the brine—
Though the sense to its revel may madly incline,
And though reason may yield to the 'hest of the heart,
'Mid the works of the builder, the triumphs of art !
But an hour, and we stand on the old rugged shore
Where the language first lisped shall be spoken once
    more,
Where the strong Anglo-Saxon makes progress and
    sign,—
Bear us with lightning speed, over the brine !

Over the brine—over the brine—
But ah, farther yet lies that dear home of mine—
The Land of the West, in which, gallant and young,
Fewer anthems, more free songs of labour are sung—
Where temples are rarer, and records more few,
And the great deeds are yet half remaining to do ;
Where the tall mountains peer and the broad rivers shine ;
Oh, to be hurried there—over the brine !

Over the brine—over the brine—
Give us quick to each other, oh Father of mine !
Me to the land that is distant and dear—
My country to me, with its destiny clear !
Over my head let the old banner wave,
When I seek for a home or sleep low in my grave !
Homeward, quick homeward, oh Father of mine,
Speed me and shelter me, over the brine !

On the British Channel, August, 1865.

THE OLD FLAG OVER-SEA.

I know not how the absence fell
    Of that, my eyes so sought with longing—
The dear old flag we loved so well
    When violent hands were wronging.

For still, thank God!—it droops and waves
    Where'er the winds of commerce woo it,
Or deed of despot, threatening slaves,
    Demands that we undo it!—

But weeks, for me, since Consul's staff
    Had shown the striped and starry streamer,
Or it had waved from frigate's gaff
    Or peak of sailing steamer.

                                 B

The meteor flag of England, here ;
 And there an ensign brighter, fuller,
And bruiting victories quite as dear—
 The Emperor's tri-colour.

It seemed to me, though dim and far
 And scarce embodied forth in thinking—
My own dear land, with stripe and star,
 To nothingness was sinking ;—

That I should know my home no more,
 However sought, through toils or dangers,—
But weary tread some foreign shore
 And live and die 'mid strangers.

And then one morn I wound my way
 Down Calton Hill of Edinboro',
With Holyrood my goal to-day
 And Stirling Carse to-morrow ;

With Arthur's Seat that skyward laughed,
 And the grim Castle piled defiant ;
Till one full cup of eld I quaffed,
 That made me feel a giant.

" Who would not stay from native land,"
    I said, "for this, so famed in story—
These memories of the Iron Hand,
    And gleams of kingly glory ! "

" Who would not ?"   Pause !—for up a spire,
    Against the blue void sheer and utter,
Azure, and white, and ruddy fire,
    I saw a banner flutter.

It was my own—*our* own !   Oh, heaven,
    How the quick throb that love convulses
When some dear recognition's given,—
    Went bounding through my pulses !

How all my native land at once
    Sprang back to being in the shimmer,
With those whose absence had for months
    Made every daylight dimmer !

The gray old driver, on his box,
    Saw the quick glance, the tear-drop starting ;
A smile, whose kin the heart unlocks,
    His sunbrowned lips was parting.

" Hech, mon !" he said, " I ken the sight
   That maks the saftenin' mood come o'er ye !
'T'is a bonnie flag ! I've seen the light
   In other eyes before ye !

" Ye'r far frae hame, and weel may spare
   Ane drap to wat ye'r country's honour ;
For sad's the load—aye, sad and sair—
   The red war's laid upon her !

" Ay, I could a'most greet, mysel',
   To see a thing so braw and bonnie,
And think what faes hae wished it ill—
   Yet floatin' high as ony ! "

I reached and grasped the driver's hand ;
   I choked with grateful, mournful feeling :
The home-flag in a foreign land
   Had brought a new revealing :

How round a simple bunting strip,
   In cost a song, in weight a feather—
A mere mouchoir for lady's.lip,—
   A nation's pride can gather !

A father's fondness for his child,
  A lover's tender, pleading passion,
A patriot's flame—to form one wild
  Unreasoning adoration.

God bless the dear old bannered fold!
  God keep the hosts who own and guard it!—
Till plucked its hues, when time is old,
  By the same Hand that starred it!

So shouted I down Calton Hill,
  And the old Gael's pleased murmur follows:
And such the shout I'll echo still,
  Upon the soil it hallows!

To float it, Western winds blow free;
  And blue bend Western skies above it;
But it needs The Old Flag Over-Sea,
  To know how much we love it!

Perthshire Highlands,
       August, 1865.

THE COMING OF MONT BLANC.

Running along the high level
　　Of Jura, wild and hard,
With the charms of the great Rhone Valley yet lingering
　　　　in my eyes,—
I heard the porter out calling
　　The station-name " Bellegarde ! "
And then in a moment later I saw wedded earth and
　　skies.

A snow-bank reached to heaven,
　　And the clouds below its crown
Seemed shrinking off from its summit in a natural fear
　　　　and awe ;—
Great feathery swales suggesting
　　The lightness of eider-down,
And held in that air-solution by nature's chemical
　　law.

And there, but a little eastward,
  Slim needles, greenly white,
Thrust up through the higher strata their points so
    fatal keen;
  Catching and breaking and changing
    The wonderful play of light,
But never losing that radiance denied to the lowlands
    mean.

The great white Alps, and their monarch,
  Mont Blanc of the royal fame,
And the Aiguillettes resplendent, that hem the robes
    of a king:
  These were the long-sought glories
    That to me that moment came;
And the hour must be far, far distant, an answering thrill
    to bring.

It seemed as if toil and danger,
  As if absence and pain and grief,
In that one supremest moment were a thousand times
    repaid—
  Like slaking the drouth of the thirsty,
    And giving the sick relief,
And allowing the tired to slumber in the cool and
    pleasant shade.

"Mont Blanc!" I cried; I remember
 How calmer companions stared
And looked, from the carriage window to see me in-
 sanely leap:
 "Mont Blanc!—Thy throne, Almighty!—
 And Thine eye its brow has dared,
As we have so often dreamed in our broken prophetic
 sleep!"

 "How far away? Is it twenty,
 Is it thirty, or fifty miles?"
And a pleasant voice makes answer, of a Swiss beside
 us there,
 While her face is lit with the calmest
 Of sweet compassionate smiles:—
 "'Tis an hundred miles from here, the great moun-
 tain heaves in air."

 An hundred miles! So reach us
 At a distance beggaring thought,
The great deeds that the wise and the mighty have
 done to exalt our race!
 So the might of the art creative,
 And the marvels it has wrought,
Outstrip the thought that is laggard and make vassals
 of time and space!

Since then, by sunlight, by moonlight,
    At soft eve and radiant morn,
I have watched the Alpine monarch and studied his
    smile and frown ;—
    Have seen moraine and glacier
      Where ice-bound rivers are born,
And passed the spot where the avalanche comes
    crashing and thundering down.

    But he gives me no hour exultant
      Like that when I seemed to choke,
On the wooded heights of Jura, with a pleasure akin
    to pain—
    When the wild white Alpine glory
      To my waiting spirit spoke,
And the scene was forever pictured on the nerves of
    heart and brain.

Interlaken, Bernese Oberland,
    July, 1867.

TWO QUEENS IN WESTMINSTER.

In the Chapel of Henry the Seventh,
  Where the sculptured ceilings rare
Show the conquered stone-work, hanging
  Like cobweb films in air,—
There are held two shrines in keeping,
  Whose memories closely press :
The tomb of the Rose of Scotland,
  And that of stout Queen Bess.

Each side of the sleeping Tudor
  They rest ; and over their dust
The canopies mould and darken
  And the gilding gathers rust ;
While low on the marble tablet,
  Each effigied in stone,
They lie,—as they went to judgment—
  Uncrowned, and cold, and alone.

Beside them pass the thousands,
    Each day; and hundreds strive
To read the whole of the lesson
    That knoweth no man alive—
Of which was more to be pitied,
    And which was more to be feared—
The strong queen, with the nerve of manhood,
    Or the woman too close endeared.

One weakened her land with faction,
    One strengthened with bands of steel;
One died on the black-draped scaffold,
    One broke on old age's wheel:
And both—oh, sweet heaven, the pity!—
    Felt the thorns in the rim of the crown
Far more than the sweep of the ermine
    Or the ease of the regal down.

Was the Stuart of Scotland plotting
    For her royal sister's all?
Was it hatred in crown or in person
    Drove the Tudor to work her fall?
Was there guilty marriage with Bothwell
    And black crime at the Kirk of Field?
And what meed had the smothered passion
    That for Essex stood half-revealed?

Dark questions!—and who shall solve them?
 Not one, till the great assize,
When royal secrets and motives
 Shall be opened to commonest eyes;—
Not even by bookworm students,
 Who shall dig, and cavil, and grope,
And keep to the ear learned promise,
 While they break it to the hope!

Ah, well—there is one sad lesson
 Made clear to us all, at the worst:
Of two forces made quite incarnate,
 And that equally blessed and cursed.
With the English woman, all-conquering
 Was Power, and its handmaid, Pride;
With the Scottish walked fierce-eyed Passion,
 Calling lovers to her side;

And the paths were the paths of ruin,
 Of disease and of woe, to both,
With their guerdon the sleepless pillow,
 And their weapon the broken troth;
And each, when she died, might have shuddered
 To know she had failed to find
A content, even poorly perfect,
 As that blessing some landless hind!

Ah, well, again—they are sleeping
    Divided, yet side by side;
And the lesson were far less perfect
    If their sepulchres severed wide.
And well for Bess and for Marie
    That the eyes, to judge them at last,
Will be free from the gloss and glamour
    Blinding ours through present and past!

Westminster Abbey,
     July, 1870.

LAKE LEMAN AND CHILLON.

At the old Genevan wharf she lay,
Where the *Jardin Anglais* looks on the bay—
   That steamer small, with a name so regal ;
Lake Leman was tempting blue, that day,
And as part of her brood we sailed away—
   Our national totem—" *L'Aigle*."

Has the world of travel a purer joy
Than the ramparts grim of old Savoy,
   As that day we sailed apast and down them ?—
Peak upon peak rising high, more high,
And some with their heads that reached the sky—
   With stern Mont Blanc to crown them ?—

With Jura's steeps on the other side
Of that lake with the dangerous placid tide ;
   And below, to the edge, the green hills sloping :
On one hand the mother, tender-eyed,
On the other the father, high in pride,
   O'er their blue-eyed darling stooping !—

With Beau Rivage, with sweet Lausanne,
With the hostel named for " milord Biron,"
   Where he heard Childe Harold's echoing thunder :
One feast to the eye, sailing on and on,
Till the cliffs hung dark over old Chillon,
   With the castle nestling under !

Time has gently dealt with the stern old pile,
And few the stones that have dropped erewhile
   From the architect's featly and graceful shaping ;
Though behind it a railway comes to spoil
The Past, with a hint of modern toil
   And a means for romance escaping.

Dark rise the old turrets—dark, yet fair,
Round tower in graceful blending with square,
   And here a tall keep over all arisen ;
Till the gazer thinks what a fortune rare
For a limited space to linger there,
   Even calling one's home a prison !

And fair as ever the sun-rays fall
On the lapping waters under the wall;
   And the view across still keeps its glory—
Over the lake to the ramparts tall,
And the great snow-mountains crowning all
   With that presence mighty as hoary.

But what dearer view was within embraced,
When over the drawbridge height we paced,
   Under the archways gray and moulding,
And stood in the midst of that stony waste
Where the hand of genius one mark has placed
   For the ages' long beholding.

Savoy's stern Dukes rule here no more:
There is silence on that presence-floor
   Where herald and king bandied feudal manners;
And the free Swiss Cantons there keep in store
Of rusty firelocks many a score
   And a dozen of red-cross banners.

And deeper within comes room on room,
Of still deepening infamy and gloom,
   Beneath and above the waters' level,—
Where the victims of old found cruel doom,
The prison a scaffold, the lake a tomb;
   And the headsman a hooded devil.

And then—the chamber of Bonnivard,
Of victims at once the evillest-starred,
   And the luckiest far, that, one summer morning
The English lord saw his place of guard,
And the old renown of the castle marred
   With a glory that came sans warning.

For who now visits the dungeons old,
But to see those " seven pillars of gothic mould,"
   With the one still bearing the broken fetters,
And the window 'neath which the blue lake rolled,
And through which the birds of lost freedom told,
   As if they were wrong's abettors?

And what, when the old pile tumbles down,
Will give to its stones their best renown?
   Some puzzling and dim historic question?
No!—the story-in-rhyme, that makes its crown,
One day at Veytaux-Chillon set down
   By a guest with a bad digestion!

Paris,
  July, 1867.

A WRAITH IN THE SCOTTISH HIGHLANDS.

Up to the North by the Highland Railway;
    And down to the South by the Great Mid-Glen—
The lake-linked canal of Caledonia,
    Historic track of her hero men;—

By the woods of Dunkeld and sweet Blair Athole,—
    By Garry's flow and Tummel's side,—
By haunted Urrard and Killiecrankie,
    Where Cavalier Claverhouse won and died;—

'Mid the orchard blooms of sunny Forres,
    Where a princely fugitive hidden lay,—
'Mong the heather-bells of the Moor of Drummossie,
    That saw red Culloden's fatal day,—

STARLIGHT. *Page* 259.

By the rushing and roaring Fall of Foyers,
  Ever singing requiems in its flow,—
By the lordly ruins of Invergarry,
  That Duke William only half laid low,—

Nay, even by storied Inverlochy,
  That is ever bright with Montrose's name,—
And through dark Glencoe, forever recalling
  The deadly assassin's sword and flame,—

What was it, through all, that walked beside me,
  Or sailed, or ran, or paused, or rode,
As if some old dim and haunting Presence
  Had been by my Highland blood bestowed?

So clear, sometimes, was its outlined seeming,
  That I half-believed *she* had grown to two—
My winsome, brown-eyed Starlight lassie,
  With her tartan-plaid and her bonnet blue.

But the face was too pale and dim with sorrow;
  Too classic the shape—the form too tall.
No—something of old it was, half-godlike,
  Like some Paladin dimmed by his coming fall.

Ah, I knew, at last ! It was *Charlie Stuart !*—
　Not as he landed on Moidart's shore,
With the memory of exiled years behind him
　And the hope of a kingdom on before;

But broken, as faithful Flora Macdonald
　Sheltered him far away in Skye ;
Rough-garbed, as when over moor and mountain
　He was forced alternate to hide and fly.

But still, ah still, the Scots-people's darling,
　The Chevalier, with his winsome smile,
And the hope of a noble and kingly future
　Though danger and want might exist the while.

What is it—I asked, when I knew the Presence
　And unbonneted stood to the princely wraith—
What is it that holds, through so many ages,
　A loyalty useless—a hollow faith ?

Ah, again came the answer—Beauty and Sorrow :
　The smile to win, with no hand to hold ;
The *might have been*, waking endless pity :
　Given these, and the wondrous secret is told.

No more, from the houses or hills they haunted,
  Go those away who have *touched the heart :*
They win what success could never win them,
  They hold what could never be held by art.

The Babes in the Tower; young murthered Arthur;
  Lady Jane, who died for an unsought crown;
The Orleans Maid, falling, madly heroic;
  The Scottish Queen by her foes crushed down;—

Ah, these have a place beyond their deserving;
  Their stories linger when brighter fade;
And on every spot where they lived and suffered
  There walks, through all coming time, a shade.

Oh, Charlie Stuart!—*poor* Charlie Stuart
  That you missed of a crown of gold and gems;
But blest, among men, to wear forever
  The proudest of mental diadems!—

To be ever loved; to be ever pitied;
  To be ever gallant and fresh and young;
To keep, through the ages, a living Presence,
  With a song and a sigh on every tongue!

Ballachulish, Western Highlands of Scotland,
      July, 1870.

HORICON.

In the midst of the mountains all bosky and wooded,
  Its bosom thick gemmed with the loveliest isles,
Its borders with vistas of Paradise studded,—
  Looking up to the heaven sweet Horicon smiles.
Thick set are its haunts with old legend and story,
  That, woven by genius, still cluster and blend;
But its beauty will cling, like a halo of glory,
  When legend and record with ages shall end.

The fleet little boats that its waters are cleaving,—
  " Hiawatha," and she of the lovelier name—
" Minnehaha "—bright fancies of Longfellow's weaving,
  May well have a place with our Horicon's fame.
Not purer their names than the flash of the waters
  That dance round the keel and that laugh round the
          prow :
Not clearer the eyes of Earth's loveliest daughters,
  Who mirrow in Horicon bosom and brow.

Far down in the waters the pebbles are gleaming—
  Far down in the clear waves that nothing can hide;
So, beauty of youth, comes the name you are dream-
      ing—
  Too pure for concealment—too gentle for pride.
So smiles on your faces the sunshine of heaven—
  The blessing distilled in the gardens of air,—
A smile of contentment from Paradise given
  That woman and lake have been fashioned so fair.

Pure Horicon! glassing the brows of the mountains,
  As handmaid might bend to a conqueror's will!—
Although nurtured and swelled by the commonest foun-
      tains,
  Yet pure, and transparent, and beautiful still!
No wonder the men of the cross and the missal
  Once named it "The Lake of the Sacrament" pure;
Or that far leagues away, from some holiest vessel,
  Its drops on the forehead could comfort and cure.

On the fair silver lake drives the Indian no longer,
  With the sweep of his paddle, the birchen canoe;
And the fortresses fall that made weakness the stronger,
  And saved the white maid when the war-whistle blew.
But 'tis well that the old and the savage are fated,
  And that danger rolls back from the Edens of earth
Our boats glide as well, with all loveliness freighted,
  And the war-whoop we lose in the sallies of mirth.

Pure Horicon! lake of the cloud and the shadow!
   Soft shimmer your moonlight and dimple your rain!
And the hearts far away—if by sea side or meadow—
   Still think of your blue with a lingering pain!
Among the far islands that glitter in heaven—
   On the dim, undiscovered and beautiful shore,—
Some glimpse of a lovelier sea may be given
   To the eyes of the perfect—but never before!

Lake George, New York,
     1860.

BEYOND TH' ATLANTIC.

Oh, friends, it is a simple phrase,
    To drive the strongest reasoner frantic—
That " Kate has gone " or " Walter stays,"
    Just now, "beyond th' Atlantic."

A measured space, that little time
    May speed the absent safely over,—
May hurry back to native clime,
    And waiting arms, the rover.

But ah, so hard to look across,
    When night falls dark, or winds are howling,
Without remembering wreck and loss
    And wild storm-demons prowling !—

So many fears must press the heart,
    When friends delay or mails are missing,—
Of fell disease's murderous dart
    Or slander's venomed hissing!

So prone the fancy is, to form
    Dark dreams of loved ones sinking, failing :
Nay, over bosoms left so warm
    Those winds in churchyards wailing!

So hard to close the mental eyes,
    To what must be, of pain and danger,
Ere on the waiting view can rise
    The dear returning stranger!

And little know the happy crowd,
    Who pass, unparted, love's existence,
Through severed ties what torments crowd
    In one broad ocean's distance.

Dear ties ; too sacred far for words!
    Sweet names that can't be lighty spoken !—
To which the heart, like love-loosed birds,
    Flies back with many a token,

As swiftly o'er three thousand miles
   Of sunny sea and foam-capped billow,
As when fond looks could answer smiles
   Bent o'er a morning pillow.

God bless them all! God keep *us* all!—
   Whether an absence short and fleeting
Is followed quick by love's sweet thrall,
   In fond and rapturous meeting—

Or weakened bolt, or failing health,
   Or heaven's decree, as blind as certain,
Beggars that mine of loving wealth
   And drops the final curtain!

Ay, His the blessing true, at last;
   For—sweetest thought to each confider!—
Though rolls th' Atlantic broad and vast,
   His sea of love is wider!

London,
   November, 1870.

ITALY, NURSE AND MOTHER!

ITALY, mother of poets!
  Nurse of the beautiful arts!
Reaching far over the ocean
  To grapple for human hearts!
Italy, mother of Tasso;
  By whose knees sad Dante sung
And Michael Angelo sculptured,
  When artist devotion was young!—

Italy, fair are thy cities,
  Where the sunshine tenderly smiles;
Fair are thy pine-clad mountains
  And lakes with their fairy isles;
And pilgrims from all the world over
  Will bend at altar and shrine,
To own what bygone glories
  And what thanks from the world are thine.

And yet, Italy, nurse and mother!
  There is something for him to say,
Who comes as an earnest pilgrim
  From a country so far away :—
Something that must be uttered,
  Even though it may seem unkind,
Like the young and the vigorous taunting
  The feeble, and old, and blind.

It is—that thy day is over,
  For leading the eager van
And teaching the needed lessons
  Of progress and truth to man !—
That the day has outrun the artist,
  And the worker takes his place,
In moulding events and actions
  For the good of the human race.

All good, in what there is left thee!
  All evil be shielded far—
With liberty's power fresh given,
  And no radical licence to mar!
So thy last days shall thy best days
  In the eyes of the Ruler be,
And the truth be proved, that 'tis never
  Too late to make men free.

Close thy dungeon doors, forever!
　　Lay the Secret tribunal by!
Let no Council of Ten, of Venice,
　　Fright the air with a murdered cry.
And cast off, though with 'bated vigour,
　　Creeds, habits, and bonds of old,
If they keep the free heart from beating
　　And leave the warm pulses cold!

But the work is with *us*, old mother!—
　　With *us*, of the Northern lands,
Where the bleak winds rave in winter
　　And the waves wash duller sands.—
With *us*, in that land far-Westward,
　　That thy true Columbus found,
And gave it to crowded Europe
　　As a wider and better ground.

Italy, nurse and mother!—
　　Greeting, warmest and best
Ever, from those who know thee,
　　In the Lands of the North and the West!
But no more expect that the sceptre
　　Leading man in his onward stride,
Will be held on the Adriatic
　　Or waved by the Tiber's side.

Venice,
　　August, 1871.

THE CROWNING FOLLY.

I sit on the deck, in mid-ocean—
    In the midst of the wild, broad sea;
While my black-winged ship o'er the billow
    Is speeding so fast and free;
And "Faster!" they cry—"go faster,
    Towards England's nearing shore!"
I only remember that distance
    Adds parting and pang the more.

And what the d—dickens—I ask it
    In the veriest shame and grief,
As I might inquire what had made me
    A branded coward and thief,—
What the dickens can be the motive,
    And what the compelling force,
Inducing a full-grown white man
    To follow so foolish a course?—

To abandon the land that is solid,
    For a sea that tumbles and heaves
Like a long perpetual earthquake
    That never raves out and leaves;
Where the bed is a bunk, never quiet,
    On the top, or the bottom, of which,
You sleep (*if* you sleep) with the comfort
    Of a horse on his back in a ditch;

Where the wind blows the hair from your caput,
    And the salt and the soot combine
To make faces as black as a kettle
    And eyes half-blinded with brine;
Where food, disdaining digestion,
    In the way that it entered, returns;
And the clouds only break, while the sunshine
    To blisters the cuticle burns;

Where you pace, like a striped hyena,
    Up and down the floor of a cage,
Combining all griefs and discomforts
    With a blending of fear and of rage;
Where the days are the longest on record,
    And yet nothing compared to the nights,
Of which all the blinded sensations
    Are yet worse than the daily frights;

Where you eat, to bring on dyspepsia;
  And drink, to become a tub;
And play at games that are childish;
  And gamble, at nothing the rub;
And smoke, till your hide is leather;
  And lie, as never on shore;
And flirt, with disgusting objects
  That wear padded stays, and snore;

Where you envy the whales that are blowing,
  And the porpoises running a race,
And the Mother Carey's chickens,—
  That at least keep their natural place;
And think, with a sort of envy,
  Of the man who was drowned last week,
Because he is through with his troubles,
  While yours lie before, in a streak!

And this—for what? To be absent
  From all that you love the best;
To break the repose of others
  As well as your natural rest;
To leave lonely hearts behind you,
  And find new discomforts ahead,
And wish you were back with your dear ones,
  Or that they, and yourself, were dead!

T

No, thank you!—not at present
   Any more of this privilege prized
Than the whimsical fates enforce me,—
   If my mind is well advised!
Not, at least, till I learn the blessing
   Of paying a doctor's bill
For supplying me drugs and potions
   That have made me confoundedly ill!

Not, at least, till I learn that exile
   From home and from native place,
Is no longer a theme for murmurs,
   But a boon to a grateful race!—
Till I feel that the highest enjoyment
   Is setting all pains at play,
And the dearest content with loved ones
   Is discovered in going away!

Till then, as the Crowning Folly
   I must speak of this whole affair,
And confess, with the deepest of blushes,
   My bad and disgraceful share.
So we'll turn every ship to a bedlam,
   With the fools all " going to sea ; "
And one of the top-sawyer places
   Reserved every year for *me !*

Off the Irish Coast,
      June, 1871.

A TRUE CHEVALIER OF THE LEGION.

I WENT on the boat at Dover,
    To cross to the coast of France,
On a bright and sunny morning of a certain late July ;
    And at the bridge I encountered
    A man with an eagle glance,
Who forbade my smoking, aft-ward, and gave me the
    reason why.

One glance revealed the Captain
    Of that fine mail-packet boat
En Français nommé " *L'Écume*," and in English called
    the " Foam ; "
    But 'twas only on the passage,
    On the lappel of his coat,
That I saw the bright red ribbon which marked his ·
    Gallic home.—

The badge of the Legion of Honour,
    To which I always bow
As if the First Napoleon before me living stood ;—
    Though they say that the decoration
    Has grown so common, now,
That the wearer and the seër both think it little good.

Eh, well !—I cannot join them !
    For I never quite forget
Whose hand first hung the token on a battle-hallowed
        breast ;
    And I think that if I could wear it,
    For some duty nobly met,
They might keep their stars and garters, their ribauds,
        and all the rest.

" Some duty nobly met "—ay,
    The phrase has its errand here,
For such was the legend written, as I saw and read,
        that day,
    On the breast of the Dover Captain
    Who wore the riband dear—
Set down in the Book of the Legion as JEAN GUILLAUME
        JUTELET.

In that Golden Book I read it—
    The tale of forty years
Unswerving, faithful service in the active French
        Marine;—
    And that something more than duty,
        Which to common eyes appears
So capable of keeping any name forever green.

For more than a score of rescues,
    Made by his strong right arm,
Of drowning men and women and of children little and
        weak—
    For half-an-hundred of beings
        Delivered from deadly harm,
With a self-forgetful bravery no form of words can
        speak,—

For this was the token given,
    With medals nearly ten,
By an often erring and trifling but seldom ungrateful
        land:
    For this did he hold a record
        In the book of ennobled men,
And beside the great commanders have the privilege
        to stand.

Beside them ? ay, above them,
    In the list of the truly great ;
For on God's great roll the rescuer the slayer far out-
    ranks,
    And no breath that rises to heaven
    Can more soften a human fate
Than the prayers of the saved, for their friend in need,
    coming up in broken thanks.

So I thought, as I bade the Captain
    Good-bye, on Calais Pier,
With old Calais Sands, and old Calais Gates both lying
    broad in view,
    And the memories crowding closely
    Of the knightly hosts who here
At Edward's and at Henry's side displayed such derring-
    do.

Which of these, from the Black Prince Edward,
    To the man-at-arms who fell
Assaulting the gate of Calais, as a duty, without a
    hope,—
    To the Generous Twelve, who offered
    Their lives so nobly and well,
As a ransom for scores of others,—to die by the shame-
    ful rope,—

Which of these, I thought, was nobler
    Or knightlier, at his best,
In the storm of steel or javelin, defending person or
      crown,
    Than the modern type of the hero,
      Fighting Death with his brave, broad breast,
And wringing away the victims he struggled to whelm
    and drown ?

God bless the Man of the Legion—
    The Chevalier indeed—
Who so well has won his honours and so modestly bears
    their weight !
    And a thousand more grow like him,
    To know that the noblest meed
Will be found in achieving good as a means of becoming
    great !

Boulogne-sur-Mer, France,
    July 15*th,* 1873.

APRÈS LE DÉLUGE FRANÇAIS.

BROWN meets me in the *Cour d'honneur*
　　Within the Paris Grand Hotel,
Where mingled triumph and despair
　　Americans display so well;
And there he says: "Old times, you see,
　　Come back, with nothing new or strange!
Paris is what it used to be—
　　As bright, as bad, as gay—no change."

"No change!"—I let him use the phrase,
　　Without one contradicting word,
But think he might have tried, for days,
　　And found no dictum more absurd.
No change! Great heaven!—then what *is* change
　　And what are steady peace and rest,
If nothing new and nothing strange
　　In this new Paris stands confessed.

The Tuileries, the Hotel de Ville,
   The Palais Royal, shapeless heaps,
And others, where, for human weal,
   The patriot or the student weeps,—
These relics of the Commune's hour
   Are " change " enough, as one might urge ;
But something else, of tenfold power,
   Hangs low on recollection's verge.

Brown does not see it.   He, and I
   Were here, for weeks, in 'Sixty-seven,
When France's star was bright and high
   And the three colours flouted heaven,—
When to the throne of Solomon,
   From farthest climes, by land and sea,
Kings, Emperors, Commons, crowded on
   To crown the Man of Destiny ;—

When on the Champ de Mars there stood
   The typic mansions of the world,
As if by some far-sweeping flood
   Into that near connection hurled ;
And in the Palace walls were stored
   Fabrics and gems of every land,
While on through every avenue poured
   All races owning Art's command.

To-day the Champ de Mars is but
    A dull and arid ashen heap :
To-day the Emperor, closely shut
    In English vaults, keeps death's long sleep.
To-day the conqueror, rich with spoil,
    And Alsace and Lorraine his prey,
With laggard step, from France's soil
    Prepares at last to march away.

Ay, worse than this—the men of France
    To-day are drifting down a tide
That has no course but merest chance—
    That anarchy most drear and wide !—
Dreaming of freedom, all unfit ;
    Acting a despotism, throughout ;
Their legislative hall a pit
    For conflicts of a rabble rout.

To-day republican in name ;
    To-morrow—in heaven's mercy, what ?
Empire or kingdom—still the same
    Insane desire for—*what is not.*
Her tradesmen hopeless as they sell ;
    Her merchants fearful as they buy ;
Her statesmen listening treason's bell
    Or revolution's battle-cry.

Filine is dull, in mad Mabille ;
 Jacques Bonhomme shrugs, but makes no sign ;
Through St. Antoine one seems to feel
 That blood is mantling in the wine.
Such—such is France, this deluge past,
 Another coming, swift and sure ;—
All doubtful, which shall be the last,
 Or what shall die and what endure.

No, Brown !—we mark with different eyes.
 You see the Paris known of old ;
I see, half-dead, what may arise,
 And may but grow more stark and cold.
A lesson slowly, surely learned :
 We grow to be the thing we will ;
We take the wages we have earned,
 Deny, rebel, and suffer, still !

St. Cloud, (Paris)
  July, 1873.

THE TWO PASSES.

I CROSSED the Splugen, in 'Seventy-one,
    To the fair Italian plains,
And thought, when the Cardinelle Pass was won
    And I stood by its guarding chains,
Looking down a precipice sheer and stark
    Of two thousand feet in all
With the great blue Gulf, the depth to mark
    Of the Madesimo's fall,—

That nothing on earth could be half so grand
    As the Splugnerberg's southern side,
Where so many of Brunc's adventurous band
    O'er the precipice plunged and died:
That nothing in all the Land of the West
    Could so the pulses chill,
Or lay so heavy a weight on the breast
    With the awed heart standing still.

But 1 crossed the Sierra in 'Seventy-two,
   To the Californian shore ;
And I drank Cape Horn's sensation new,
   With a shudder unknown before,—
Looking down from the side of a palace-car
   Half a mile to the depth below,—
With the Sierra Nevada near and far
   Thrusting up its peaks of snow.

And then I said : this is grander yet
   Than the Alpine pass so wild,
And the Western World can never forget
   To be Nature's favourite child :
To show bluer skies, and streams more broad,
   And peaks still highest in air,
Bearing up the mind to the might of God
   With the very shudder of prayer.

To-day I sit where neither is seen—
   Cape Horn or the Cardinelle ;
But the memory of both is fresh and green
   And they balance each other well.
And I say : God's hand in every land
   Strews wonders for those who see,
And the last will always be doubly grand
   To enthusiast fools like me !

London,
   August, 1873.

AT THE GOLDEN GATE.

Years, years of waiting, while in shapes terrific
    Have loomed the obstacles that held me back;
And now I see, at length, the broad Pacific
    Rolling far westward in the sunset's track;
And now I know how that discoverer Spanish,
    Balboa, his long toilsome journey made,
One first glimpse caught, in fear the whole might vanish,
    A mirage,—dropped upon his knees and prayed.

The Sunset Sea!   The noblest and the broadest
    Of all the oceans girdling wave-washed earth;
The calmest, gentlest, yet at times the maddest,
    In raving paroxysms of stormy mirth.
The Eagle's continent its eastern border;
    Its western, that on which one-half mankind
Sit under despotisms of deadly order
    And bow to superstitions old as blind.

And yet how near together, spite of distance,
 Stand the two mighty continents, to-day !
How nearly, at this stage of man's existence,
 Current to current makes its powerful way !
Within this Golden Gate, the noblest, surely,
 Of all the entrances of all the seas,
The Asian barks-of-hope float in securely,
 And furl their lateen sails, and ride at ease.—

To prove that land to land is each a neighbour,
 Though leagues unnumbered stretch between the
   twain ;
To complicate the problem vexed, of labour,
 And aid, one day, perhaps, to make it plain ;
While westward stretches, to the Orient boundless,
 An influence mighty, from the Land of Gold,
Of which no hope can e'er be vain or groundless
 Till all the New has leavened all the Old.

The Golden Gate, indeed !—where cliffs stand sentry,
 And mountains heavenward lift their giant forms,
And western gales make rough and dangerous entrée
 To havens that shut away the wildest storms,—
Fit index for the marvellous City, rising
 To granite strength from whelming waves and sands,—
In wealth, in vice, in power, in good, surprising,—
 Most strange anomaly of human hands !

The Golden Gate, indeed !—when morning flashes
  Its cloudless splendours o'er wave, cliff, and height,—
When wild the surf on rocky Lobos dashes—
  Then glorious, grand, exhilarant and bright ;
But crowned supreme, when cloudland's shapes immortal
  Attend the sun low down the radiant west,
And the grand gateway grows a gilded portal
  For sailing towards the Islands of the Blest.

San Francisco, California,
    June, 1872.

OIRISH GLIMPSES.

Dialect Sketches, after the manner of the
" Groves o' Blarney."

I.

THE LANDING AT QUEENSTOWN.

'MID haltings and rushings,
And pokings and pushings,
The New Yorruk stamer, one summer day,
The Cove o' Cork in
Was disembarkin'
The visitors foine for the Jim av the Say.

Ony list would be taydious,
And slightly invayjus,
Av the quality hoigh, wid the gold galore,
Who the skein av their travel
Did then unravel,
On the Oirish turf by stheppin' ashore.

U

And, more be token,
Let the truth be sphoken—
The list would be broken, if great or small ;
For some didn't mingle, and
Went on to England,
And the same didn't land at all at all.

But the rest—they landed,
And not empty-handed,
Wid directions bandied in Babel's tongues ;
And the landing was asy,
In the stame-tug, whazy
Be rayson av cowld in her iron lungs.

Well, they trod the ould soil, thin,
Wid wondher and smoile, thin,
Till the paylers came down to examine the thrunks ;
Then (fwhat tyranny this tells !)
Sure they sayzed all the pistils,
And the gowld for the Faynians, in ingots and chunks !

Then, when searched to the bottom,
The donkey-boys got 'em,
And on baggage-carts put 'em, wid scrubs to the fore,
So little and thrifling
That, if sthock they wur rifling
Aich trunk would have held its two donkeys or more.

But fwhat matther for size, sure,
Whin around thim the byes, sure,
Belaboured wid noise, sure, and pounded wid sthicks ?—
Wid their : " Wud yez go aan, now ! "
" Sure the place is nigh haan', now ! "
" Yer banner, faix Micky's the divil for thricks ! "

But not Nebuchadnayzar,
Nor Julius Caysar,
Nor no man of their day, sir, could iver compare
Wid the royal attindance
That did just begin thince
To follow the travellers wid anxious care.

There was Mrs. Moloney's
Self, and dozen of cronies,
All moany and groany's the dismallest day ;—
Wid the collars av linen,
And swate broidery-holes grinnin',
And handkerchiefs thin in the hand to display.

There was Mrs. O'Blaggard,
And tin others more haggard,
Wid the bog-wood all cut in the rarest av shapes—
Bracelets, breast-pins and ear-rings,
Napkins, breakfast and tea-rings,
And castles and abbeys and bunches o' grapes.

Thin, the beggars on crutches,
And ould women in mutches,
Wid the tinderest touches in prayer and whine,—
Mingled blessings and curses,
Till they drew all the purses,
Or instead (which much worse is) some words I decline!

*　　　*　　　*　　　*　　　*

Och, Queenstown, me jewel!—
There's nothing you do ill;
But your best to the wurruld is quite onbeknownst:
You save visiting strangers
From all future dangers
By making thim beggars and idjuts at wanst!

II.

THE SIEGE OF BALVELLY.

Faix, a foine ould ruin,
Past Time's ondoin',
Balvelly Castle o'erlooks the Lee;
And men often wondher,
When standin' ondher,
Fwhat the name av the founder may chance to be.

But av late, wid learning
A rich salary earning
From the hands discerning that scatter the gowld,—
One has cleared the mystery
That wrapped its history,
And the name and the fame av the builder tould.

It was built—he said it,
And faix we must credit
The man who drank the Pyaerian Spring,—
Sthicking up o'er the tide, yet,
Av the Flood, not dried yet,
As the hunting-box av an Oirish King.

Phelim Shawn Macnamâra
Macmurtough O'Hara
Ruadh Dermot O'Callaghan Shamus O'More
Patrick Feargus McCarty
Was the royal ould party,
Though his names, faix, I disremimber a score.

He was moighty and foine, then,
And the tenth av his loine, then;
And a thousand armed servants awaited his call,—
That is, they pretinded,
And there it all ended,
For the sorra a wan came at all at all.

So that whin his big brother—
King, av coorse, and another
Long tail av the O's and the Mores and Macs,—
Said he'd threated his daughter
As no wan had oughter,
And he'd batther his pig-pen and bate him like wax,—

Then the King, wid that spirit
The Celts inherit,
Cut the lady's head off, widout delay,
Hung it out for a banner,
And said, in that manner :
" I'm agreeable, ould one—batther away !"

So he did—the besager,
A rig'lar ould stager,
Who had stholen and fought for three wives av his
own ;—
Swearin' by that and by this mass,
That betune then and Christmas
He'd not lave av the castle wan sthone upon sthone.

But though deadly his foray,
'Twasn't done in a hurry—
The takin' that place, while the whiskey held out—
Wid aich rough galligaskin
That kilt wid no askin',
And bogtrotters there wid their spirits so stout.

Wan by wan, though, they perished,
Retainers so cherished
(On all they could asily grab at or steal) ;
Dying, while they could swig it,
Wid mouth at the spigot,
Or fightin' inside, for the gineral weal.

But at last the McCarty,
Wid his courage so hearty,
Countin' up where his henchmen so low were laid,—
Seeing life in no more of 'em,
And dead some six score of 'em,
Remarked : " Tare an' ages !—but this thing is played ! "

Thin wid a swate smile, he
Made an illegant pile he
Well knew to be powdher, and sittin' on top,
Touched it off wid the poker ;
And faix the ould joker
Wint up through the roof wid a beautiful pop !

F'where he wint, who can tell us ?
For those noice ould fellows
Have ways that meself can't measure, bedad !
And the priest had just shrived him,
And somewhat un-wived him ;
And may be a passage right upward he had.

More be token, his body—
Now wasn't it odd, he
Had much av it !—niver was found, hide or hair ;
And so the impression
Is safe as confession,
That he wint—well, we can't say exactly where.

But the Castle : th' explosion
Caused a bit of erosion
That left it no roof and but moderate walls ;
So that whin they'd taken it,
Ivery sthone did shake in it,
And the worth wasn't much, for baronial halls.

But his daughter, in segments
And very small fragments,
The father bereaved gathered up in a hod,
And wid tin thousand curses,
Mixed wid funeral verses,
Left Balvelley a place for the bat and the tod.

Still the travellers see, there,
Rising over the Lee, there,
Balvelly Castle, so ould and so grand ;
But they miss the big sthory
That makes its glory,
And they'll scarcely belave it whin tould off-hand.

III.

Killarney from the Kenmare Road.

Och, what beauties broke on us,
What glories won us,
And how ivery lip broke out into cries,
Whin, as evening was nearing,
We saw the appearing
Av Killarney's mountains, wathers and skies!

How the west-light ruddy
On Magillicuddy,
Made the rough and craggy all gentle and sweet!
How there seemed a fountain
On Purple Mountain,
For the very bathing av angels' feet!

How the dim Black Valley
Made the courage rally,
In thinking av midnight spells and av storms,—
And the frightened quiver
That would make one shiver,
Meeting there wid a few av the ghostly forms!

Thin, how softly and sweetly,
At peace completely,
The Lakes themselves lay taking their rest,—
Wid the isles av splendour
On aich bosom tindher,
As if aich was holding her babes to her breast !

Och, Killarney !—cluster
Av all glories that musther
In ivery land, oudher ivery sky !—
We may meet your aiqual
In some happy sayquel ;
But niver, bedad !—till we've learned to fly !

IV.

TWO FUNERALS AT GLASNEVIN.

Glasnevin—Glasnevin !
Where the sad bereavin'
Av many a heart, makes richer the ground ;
Where the loved ones they bury
Chill the heart that is merry,
And the silence is sadder than mournfullest sound.

Sure we saw at the gate, thin,
Fwhat tould av the fate, thin.
Av all who walk on humanity's road—
Two classes of mortal,
At one narrow portal,
Comin' in, to take up their unconscious abode.

Wid the wan, men in dozens,
Friends, brothers, and cousins,
Well dressed, rode and walked by the rich-plumed
hearse ;
While a preacher, in sable,
Wid white linens, was able
O'er the dead to tell flatherin' truths (may-be worse !)

Wid the odher, a woman,
Clothed dingy and common ;
A coffin av deal, on two shoulthers av men.
Not av mourners the laste, see !
And only the praste, see,
Walkin' first, wid' a power av grief in his ken.

Then a sad old ballad
To the memory rallied,
Long ago set down when two opposites died ;
And there rose up the prayer, too,
That had been uttered there, too ;
"May their souls, at the Judgment, not sever as wide!"

But the lime-tree breath, there,
Made the thought av death, there,
Less gloomy and sad than on many a sod;
And we marked, ungrieving,
That moment, when leaving,
Glasnevin true part of the " Acre of God."

V.

THE JAUNTING CAR.

Och, spirit av Pindar,
Wid no wan to hindher,
Make me fancy like tindher to catch the flame,—
While I sing, of ould Erin,
The thing most cheerin'—
The jaunting car—faix, but I mane that same!

Fwhat was Oireland without it?
A mistake—who can doubt it?—
A desert, like Aigypt or swindling Greece;
And the Roman chariot,
Wid high hand might carry it,
But the Oirish car bears us the Golden Fleece.

Wid its nate, soft cushions,
That need holdin's and pushin's,
And an arm, sometimes, round the daintiest waist;
Wid the driver young Dennis,
Or the bye Maginnis,
That would niver look back—no, sorra a taste!

Wid the seats out-turning,
For the scenery learning,
And a shelf below for the sole av the fut;
And an apron over,
The nate limbs to cover,
Like the jewels in caskets all closely shut.

Och, arrah, me honey!—
That's the ride for the money,
Wid a Kerry pony at gallop or throt,—
Wid the sun above us,
And the girruls that love us,
And a thrifle widin us av something hot!

Och, Kathleen, me beauty!—
Sthep out to yer duty!—
The gintry's behind yez—thry what yez can do!—
A mile in a minute,
Or the bad luck is in it,—
Forbye takin' time for a tumble or two!

And the man who has thried it,
And then will deride it—
Faix, there's nothing for him, aid his sthony ould
      heart,
But the one dhrive to suit him,
To the place where they shoot him,
Or up to the limb av a tree, on a cart!

VI.

A Visit to Blarney.

Swate ould Blarney Castle,
That wid cent'ries could wrastle,
And Cromwell asself, widout fallin' in hapes,—
    Sure there's pains and there's pleasures,
    Explorin yer treasures,
That sorra a wan av yer lovers escapes.

Faix, the ould woman's thratement,
Widout any abatement,—
We treasure it duly and think av it long:
    How she loudly insisted
    That the bowlder we kissed, it
Was the Blarney·adself, all lovely and sthrong.

How she foamed and she spluttered,
And benisons muttered,
Betune the two turns av an illegant cough,
Bekase (fatal stop av it!)
No one went to the top av it
And made the attimpt to fall quietly off!

How the quare ould fiddler,
And ha'penny wheedler,
Wid following av urchins most numerous to see,—
Led up from the Village,
Wid prospects av pillage,
Playin' over " The Groves," keyed at fiddle-de-dee!

How the fleas and the beggars
(The latter long-leggers)
Hung fast av the car, more tighter nor glue ;
And not wan out av breath for it,
Though runnin' to death for it,
Wid their " Now, sir, a ha'penny !"—manin' two.

Och, Blarney, ma bouchal !—
No risidence ducal,
Can show half the charm av your Castle and Groves ;
But the fact I'm expressing
Is, we'd double yer blessing,
Widout fleas by the million and beggars in droves !

In the Irish Mountains,
June, 1870.